"I know exa...

Something in the way Morgan said those words heated her blood. Was she imagining things, or had his voice dropped suggestively lower when he'd made the statement?

"I need to know your likes and dislikes," Lena said, after a calming, deep breath. "I'd like to ask you some questions," she said.

"Ask away."

"Are you interested in a single-story or two-story structure?"

"Two-story."

She nodded as she jotted the information down. "How about a swimming pool?"

"Umm. Do you swim, Lena?"

She looked up, surprised by his question. "Yes."

Morgan nodded. "Then I'd like a pool and a nice yard. It really doesn't matter how big the living room is as long as the house has a large master bedroom. That's where I plan to spend most of my time."

Figures, she thought, jotting the information down. Lena couldn't resist the image that suddenly flashed through her mind. It was a vision of a sleeping Morgan, naked and tangled in silken sheets...

Books by Brenda Jackson

Kimani Romance

Solid Soul
Night Heat

Silhouette Desire

*Delaney's Desert Sheikh #1473
*A Little Dare #1533
*Thorn's Challenge #1552
Scandal Between the Sheets #1573
*Stone Cold Surrender #1601
*Riding the Storm #1625
*Jared's Counterfeit Fiancée #1654
Strictly Confidential Attraction #1677
Taking Care of Business #1705
*The Chase Is On #1690
*The Durango Affair #1727
*Ian's Ultimate Gamble #1756

*Westmoreland family titles

BRENDA JACKSON

is a die "heart" romantic who married her childhood sweetheart and still proudly wears the "going steady" ring he gave her when she was fifteen. Because she's always believed in the power of love, Brenda's stories always have happy endings. In her real-life love story, Brenda and her husband of thirty-three years live in Jacksonville, Florida, and have two sons.

A *USA TODAY* bestselling author, Brenda divides her time between family, writing and working in management at a major insurance company. You may write Brenda at P.O. Box 28267, Jacksonville, Florida 32226, by e-mail at WriterBJackson@aol.com or visit her Web site at www.brendajackson.net.

BRENDA JACKSON

Beyond Temptation

KIMANI
ROMANCE

To Gerald Jackson, Sr.,
my husband, hero and best friend.

To my readers who have been
waiting patiently for Morgan's story.

To my Heavenly Father who gave me the gift to write.

And lead us not into temptation...
—*Matthew* 6:13

 KIMANI PRESS™

ISBN-13: 978-0-373-86000-5
ISBN-10:   0-373-86000-5

BEYOND TEMPTATION

Copyright © 2007 by Brenda Streater Jackson

www.kimanipress.com

Printed in U.S.A.

Dear Reader,

For all of those cynics that don't believe in true love, I say, "Of course there is a soul mate out there for everyone, and no one should settle for anything less!"

For example, take the case of Helena (Lena) Spears. I know people like Lena, and I'm sure you do, too. Lena lovingly takes on the role of primary caretaker for her elderly mother. She never has time for herself, and because of her family obligations, she has dating "challenges." After many disappointments, Lena gives up on finding a man who will accept, support and love her.

And although she doesn't know it at first, Morgan Steele is just the man that Lena needs—if only she could open her heart, mind and soul to what he is offering. But never fear, because Morgan is a Steele. And what Morgan wants, Morgan is determined to get.

I hope you enjoy reading how Morgan and Lena work through their issues and discover what is waiting for them beyond temptation.

Brenda Jackson

Acknowledgements

To Gerald Jackson, Sr., my husband, hero and best friend. To my readers who have been waiting patiently for Morgan's story. To my Heavenly Father who gave me the gift to write.

And lead us not into temptation

Matthew 6:13

Chapter 1

"Mr. Steele, your two o'clock appointment has arrived."

Morgan Steele's pulse immediately kicked up a notch with his secretary's announcement. He inhaled deeply and deliberately cleared his mind of everything except the woman who was about to walk into his office. Helena Spears.

"Give me a few minutes, Linda, before sending her in."

"Yes, sir."

After clicking off the line he stood and threw the

papers he'd been reading into his briefcase before snapping it shut and inwardly telling himself to relax. Getting Helena to his office had been the first hurdle, and he was determined to make it over the rest. He was smart enough to know that if at first you don't succeed you try again, and today he was a man with a more defined plan.

Putting his briefcase aside he found himself glancing toward the door, his pulse kicking up another notch as he remembered the night—a little more than a year ago—when he had first seen her as she walked into that charity ball wearing a very sexy fuchsia-colored dress. There had been something about her entrance that had momentarily taken his breath away, left him awestruck, mesmerized. And moments later when he had gazed into the warmth of her cinnamon-brown eyes, he had felt it. It had happened just the way he'd known it would once he found her—the perfect woman he had been holding out for all these years.

The only thing that hadn't happened as he'd assumed it would was her acceptance. Lena, as she was known to her family and friends, wasn't seeing things quite his way. She'd tried to explain to him, in a nice way and more than once, that she wasn't interested in a man-woman relationship of any kind.

She liked her life just the way it was and had no intentions of wasting her time indulging in a meaningless affair. Nor, she'd gone further on to add, was she interested in a meaningful one, either. She had been there, done that, and she'd learned a valuable lesson and had no intentions of doing a repeat.

All that was well and good but she wasn't dealing with any regular man. At thirty-three he could admit to being arrogant, methodical and unwilling to bend in his pursuit of anything. Once he saw something he wanted and made a decision to have it, he refused to give up until he got it.

And the bottom line was that he wanted Lena.

He had wasted enough time and starting today he intended to use a different approach. He glanced toward the door again when he heard the sound of the knob turning. The moment it opened and his "perfect" woman walked in he couldn't help but release a breath. He felt the sizzle as heat shimmered all through him. She was wearing a periwinkle-color business suit and she looked good in it.

"Lena, please come in," he said cordially as his gaze floated over the rest of her with an analytical eye. She had just the right amount of makeup on her strikingly attractive medium brown face, which placed emphasis on the honey brown curls that flowed around her shoulders, giving her the appearance of a Queen Latifah look-alike.

She was five feet ten, just the right height for his six-three stature. Her body was stacked, well endowed in all the right places, full breasts, wide child-bearing hips, voluptuous thighs and the most gorgeous pair of shapely legs he'd ever seen on a woman. He'd once overheard a conversation she'd had with his sister-in-law Kylie, who happened to be her best friend, about what she thought was a weight problem. As far as he was concerned, she didn't have one. When he looked at her, what he saw was a full-figured, thirty-one-year-old attractive and desirable woman who could start anything and everything inside him to stirring. The woman was temptation at its finest; however, when it came to her he was prodded to look beyond temptation and see something a lot more lucrative and worthwhile. Little did she know but he intended to open up a whole new world for the both of them.

"Thank you, Morgan," she said, closing the door behind her, and breaking into his thoughts. "I'm here for our two o'clock appointment."

From the sound of things she intended to be all business, and that was okay for now. He would give her this time because in the coming weeks he intended to get his. She would find out soon enough that she had just walked into a "Steele cage" and there was no way out. He had failed at plan A, but he had just put plan B into full motion.

Lena pressed her lips firmly together as she looked across the room at the man leaning against his desk. Morgan Steele.

She thought the same thing now that she did that night she'd first met him. He had to be the most gorgeous human male to grace this planet, which prompted her to put her guard up even more. The last thing she needed in her life was a man, especially one like Morgan. She'd learned her lesson a few years ago that when it came to "pretty boys" and "fine as a dime" men, she had to watch her step.

But still…although she tried not to stare but couldn't help herself. She'd been attracted to him from the first. Maybe it was the beautiful coloring of his skin, which reminded her of deep rich chocolate. Or it could have been the long lashes and dark eyes. And heaven forbid if she left out the chiseled jaw, high cheekbones, low-cut black hair and a pair of lips that were too provocative to be attached to any mouth.

The first night they'd met he'd surprised her by coming on to her and asking her out. She had turned him down flat. To this day she really didn't know why he'd bothered since men who looked like him didn't go for Amazons. They were usually seen with the slim, willowy, model types. Evidently, once she'd turned him down he'd seen her as a challenge and had asked her out several times after that. But each time she would decline. Finally, she had felt the need to put an end to whatever game he was playing by explaining her position on dating to him. She was too caught up in other things she considered more important than to be added to another man's list as his flavor for the month.

As with any potential client she had done her research, which really hadn't been necessary since Morgan's oldest brother, Chance, had married her best friend, Kylie, over a year ago. Besides, most people who'd lived in these parts for a relatively long period of time knew about those four Steele brothers who ran their family business, the Steele Corporation.

Chance at thirty-seven was CEO. Sebastian Steele, nicknamed Bas, who had gotten married just a few weeks ago, was thirty-five and the corporation's problem solver and troubleshooter. Morgan was thirty-three and headed the research and development department of the company; and Donovan, at thirty-one, headed the product development division.

Then there were the three female cousins of whom only one—Vanessa—worked in the company as head of PR. The other two, Taylor and Cheyenne, had established careers outside of the family business but maintained positions on the board of directors.

"May I offer you something to drink, Lena? Springwater, juice, coffee?"

Morgan's question pulled her thoughts back in and she licked her suddenly dry lips and tightened her hand on her briefcase as if it were her block of strength. "No, thanks," she said, moving closer into the room. "And since you're a busy man I'm sure you want us to get right down to business."

"Yes, I prefer that we do since I have another meeting in about an hour."

She nodded, glad they were on one accord. She hadn't known what to expect when he'd set up the appointment. From past encounters she assumed he was a laid-back sort of guy. It was refreshing to know he could be strictly business when the situation called for it.

"Would you like to have a seat so we can get started?" he asked, pushing away from the desk and pulling her thoughts back on track.

"Yes, thanks," she said, forcing the words out from a constricted throat. He was dressed in a business suit that made him look like he belonged on the cover of an issue of *Sexy Man* magazine. She took the seat in front of his desk, and as soon as she sat down she noted once she tilted her head up she had a direct aim to his face, specifically his *let-me-seduce-you* dark eyes.

A sensuous shiver glided down her spine when their eyes met. She cleared her throat, determined to stay on track. "I understand you're interested in purchasing another home," she said to get the conversation going.

"Yes, I am and you come highly recommended."

She couldn't help the smile that curved her lips. "By Kylie?"

He chuckled. "Yes, her too, but I would expect that since she's your best friend. Actually the person who's been singing your praises has been Jocelyn. According to her, you found her and Bas the perfect house."

Lena chuckled. "Finding the right home for Jocelyn was easy. She knew exactly what she wanted."

"Then I should be easy as well since I know exactly what I want, Lena."

There was something about the way Morgan had said the words that had heat flowing hot and heavy through her bloodstream. Was she imagining things or had his voice dropped just a little when he'd made the statement? Deciding she was imagining things she took a deep breath and said, "I need to know your likes and dislikes, and to find those things out there're a series of questions I need to go through to make sure we're on the same page as to what you're looking for in a home." She reached for the briefcase she had placed by her chair, opened it and pulled out a tablet.

"Ready?" she asked, glancing back up at him.

"Yes, ask away," he said, moving around his desk to take the chair behind it.

"Okay. Are you interested in a single-story or a two-story structure?"

"Two-story."

She nodded as she jotted the information down. "Do you anticipate doing a lot of entertaining?"

"Why?"

She glanced up. "Because if you are, you might want to consider a home with a courtyard, a swimming pool or a larger-than-normal living room area."

"Umm, I have a swimming pool at my present home so I'd want to purchase a house with another one. Do you swim, Lena?"

She looked surprised by his question. "Yes."

He nodded. "I'd like another pool and a nice yard. It really doesn't matter how big the living room is as long as the house has a nice-size bedroom. That's where I plan to spend most of my time."

Figures, she thought, jotting the information down. She couldn't help the visual that suddenly flashed through her mind of a sleeping Morgan tangled in silken sheets. "What about the size of the kitchen?"

"What about it?"

She tried not to roll her eyes to the ceiling. "Do you cook a lot? If so, then you might want a home with a large kitchen."

He shrugged. "No, I don't plan on spending a lot of time in the kitchen but my wife might."

She lifted her head from the paper and met his gaze. "Wife?"

"Yes, or perhaps I should say future wife."

"Are congratulations in order?"

"No. But I'm making sure I cover all bases since I don't intend to move again. Whoever becomes the future Mrs. Morgan Steele will be moving into that house with me."

"What if she doesn't like the decor?"

"Then she's free to change it."

Lena nodded. "What about your present home?"

"I want you to sell it."

"All right. Anything other than the swimming pool and large bedroom that you're looking for in the new house? Do you have a preference for carpet or wood floors?"

Again he shrugged. "Doesn't matter to me. Which do you suggest?"

She shrugged her own shoulders. "Either is fine, it's a matter of taste."

"All right, I guess you can show me both."

"That won't be a problem. Now, for your present home, I would need to see it and I prefer that you're there with me when I do."

"Why?"

"So you can point out some things about it that I might overlook, key selling points. We can do a tour and you can tell me things you like most about your house that might hook an interested buyer."

"Okay, you can arrange a date and time with my secretary," he said, trying not to sound too anxious. "I'm flying out tomorrow on a business trip and won't be back until the end of the week."

"That's fine and I'll get on this right away."

"Thanks, I'd appreciate it."

She stood and glanced over at him. "Any particular time frame you're aiming for to be in your new home?"

"Not particularly. How long do you think it will take?" he asked, coming to his feet as well.

"I don't anticipate it taking long. There are several new subdivisions going up around Charlotte. Is there a certain price range I need to stay in?"

"No. If it's something I want, then I intend to get it."

Another heated sliver passed down her spine with his comment. It seemed he had been looking directly in her eyes when he'd made the statement, but of course she knew she was again imagining things after studying his impassive expression. "All right, then. I'll be in touch when you return. I hope you have a nice trip."

"Thanks."

She gathered her briefcase and headed for the door.

"Lena?"

She glanced back over her shoulder. "Yes?"

"How's your mother?"

Lena couldn't help but smile. No matter when she saw Morgan, he was always kind enough to inquire about her mother. "Mom is fine. Thanks for asking."

"You're welcome."

Lena quickly made it to the door. Without looking back she opened it and stepped out, grateful for her escape. She could handle only so much heat shivering down her spine.

When Lena made it to her car she leaned back against the seat, letting her neck relax against the headrest before snapping her seat belt in place. She had been in Morgan's presence less than thirty minutes, but from the way her heart was beating it seemed longer.

There were times when a part of her longed not to be the responsible and sensible person she was. Every once in a while she was tempted to become her Gemini twin, the one who wasn't the good girl; the one who wouldn't hesitate to let her hair down, throw caution to the wind and walk boldly on the wild side. And the first thing she would do is take on a man like Morgan Steele and see if she could hold her own with him. Just the thought of having a one-night stand to feed the sudden, intense hunger she would get whenever she watched a romantic movie, or indulged in those romance novels her secretary would pass on to her, made her breasts tingle.

If she ever became her wannabe mischievous twin, that meant having the courage to trade her sensible four-door sedan in for that two-seater convertible she always wanted—and turning her nighttime fantasies into reality by behaving in such a way that would blow a fuse just thinking about. She didn't want to dwell on all the naughty pleasures she would have.

Lena immediately dismissed the thoughts of her less than sensible twin, knowing she could never do anything like that. Her life was what it was and she couldn't change it. She wasn't the mischievous twin, she was the good one who had responsibilities that took precedence over anything else, including her desire to have Morgan Steele in her bed. Her mother came first.

She was her mother's sole caretaker and had

been since her father's death six years ago. Her mother's health began failing her soon after her husband passed, making it hard for her to get around at times. A part of Lena believed it was due more to loneliness than anything else because a lot of her mother's problems were more emotional, especially the bouts of depression.

Her parents had had a rather close marriage and Lena was born after they had already been happily wedded for close to twenty years. A number of miscarriages had convinced her parents they would spend the rest of their lives childless, and Lena had been a big surprise to her forty-three-year-old father and her forty-year-old mother.

Growing up in the Spears household, she had always felt loved and cherished by her parents and she missed her father dearly. For that reason she clearly understood the depth of loss her mother felt and the bouts of occasional depression that had followed. Even now on occasion, Lena would wake up during the night and hear her mother calling out for her father in her sleep, and it always brought tears to Lena's eyes that anyone could have loved someone that deep and strong. It was on those nights after getting her mother settled back down that she would acknowledge the depth of her own loneliness and restlessness and give in to her fantasies of Morgan.

She inhaled deeply as she started her car. She glanced at the clock on the dashboard. In a few hours it would be time to pick her mother up from the adult day care. She went there twice a week for social enrichment and interaction on the recommendation of her mother's social worker. Although it had put a huge dent in her budget, so far it had been a month and Lena hadn't received a call from the day care's director letting her know her mother had begun withdrawing, which usually was a clear sign that she was headed for another bout of depression.

Lena smiled thinking she had an idea as to why. Her mother had been talkative a lot lately when Lena had picked up her, and had told her about Ms. Emily, a newcomer to the day care. It seemed that she and Ms. Emily, who was also a widow in her early seventies, had struck up a friendship and Lena was glad about that. Her mother was someone who didn't warm up to people easily.

And speaking of warming up…she allowed her thoughts to return to Morgan. Everything about him spoke of the dynamics of a man who was used to having his way. Well, unfortunately, she had shown him the few times he'd come on to her that she wasn't putty in any man's hand. The only thing the two of them could ever share was friendship. And after her last serious talk with him about three months ago, he hadn't asked her out again, so she could only assume that he'd finally gotten the message if today was anything to go by. He had acted strictly business.

The last few men she'd fancied herself as possibly having a serious relationship with had painstakingly informed her that as long as she came with extra baggage—namely her elderly mother—no man in his right mind would be interested in marrying her.

She had decided if that was the case, then she would live the rest of her life single and not worry about indulging in a committed relationship because she and Odessa Spears were a package and would remain as such until their dying days.

Deciding she didn't want to spend the rest of the day thinking about the things she would never have, she shifted her thoughts to the things that she could have—namely a big sale if she located Morgan the house he wanted, and if she sold the one he now owned. Pulling off such a feat would pay a hefty commission and she would do her best getting him just what he wanted. And she knew exactly what she would do with the money. She would get her mother involved in even more enrichment programs for senior citizens as well as plan a cruise for the both of them. It had been a while since they'd gone on a vacation together, and it was time that they did.

"You're late, Morgan. You know I don't like keeping Shari waiting."

Morgan slid into the booth across from his brother and glanced up into Donovan's annoyed features and rolled his eyes. "Shari today, Kari tomorrow, whatever. Besides, it couldn't be helped. I had an important meeting that I needed to keep."

Morgan glanced around. The Racetrack Café was a popular place in town to grab something to eat and to wet your lips with a drink. Owned by several race car drivers on the NASCAR circuit, it had become one of Donovan's favorite hangouts mainly because his best friend, Bronson Scott, was now one of the drivers on the NASCAR circuit.

Donovan finished off what was left of what he was drinking. "So you did have your meeting with Lena?"

Morgan frowned. "How did you know about our meeting?"

Donovan gave his brother one of his cocky smiles that was known to grate on his nerves before motioning for the waiter to bring him another drink. "To answer your question, I knew something was up with you this morning at the meeting in Chance's office. Most of the time you sat there like you were zoned out. I figured you either had had a rather good night or you were finally putting together a solution to your problem."

They paused in conversation long enough for the waiter to drop Donovan another drink off and to take Morgan's order before Morgan turned narrowed eyes back to his brother. "My problem?"

Donovan chuckled. "Yeah, and don't play dumb. All of us know how you have the hots for Lena Spears."

The hots didn't come close to covering it, Morgan thought, leaning back in his seat. However, Donovan, who didn't yet know the meaning of one woman for one man, was the last person who needed to know that. "And just who is all of us?"

Donovan grinned. "Me, Chance and Bas, mainly. We're the ones who've been putting up with your bad-ass moods since meeting the woman. Some days you act like it's our fault that she's not interested in you."

Morgan didn't like Donovan's assumptions. "She is interested."

"Could have fooled me. In fact she's doing a good job of fooling a lot of people since she hasn't given you the time of day. How many times has she turned you down for a date, Morgan?"

"None of your damn business." The waiter placed his beer in front of him and it was right on time, Morgan thought, taking a swallow straight from the bottle. It was either that or smashing Donovan's face in.

"Well, you know how I feel about any man running behind a woman. Downright disgusting. It should be the other way around," Donovan said, taking a sip of his drink. "And I understand you're going out of town for a few days to hang out with Cameron in Atlanta. I'm sure sometime during your visit the two of you will have a pity party since he's just as messed up over Vanessa as you are with Lena."

Morgan's features grew dark as he glanced across the table at Donovan. "Cameron and I are meeting to discuss a business venture we're both interested in and not for any damn pity party." When Donovan merely shrugged Morgan felt the need to add "I hope I'm around when you suffer your first heartbreak."

"Sorry to disappoint you but it won't happen. There isn't that much woman in the world, Morgan. Why settle for just one when the world is filled with so many of them? And now that the Steele Corporation has signed on as one of Bronson's sponsors for NASCAR, and I get to go to many of the races, the pickings are even better. I never knew so many good-looking women were interested in fast cars. Man, if you could only see them. They look just as good with their clothes on as they do with them off. There's this one sista who has a tattoo on her—"

"Hey, spare me the details, Donovan," Morgan said, holding up his hand.

"You don't know what you're missing."

Morgan shook his head. "Trust me, I believe I do."

Donovan leaned back in his chair and rubbed his chin as he studied Morgan. Within a year's time two of his brothers had made it to the altar, and it seemed Morgan was hell-bent on making it three. He liked his sisters-in-law true enough and was happy for his brothers, but his dream girl was one who was no more interested in marriage than he was. Like him the only thing she was interested in was a good time.

"So tell me, Morgan, why did you want to meet here instead of back at the office?"

"Does there have to be a reason?" Morgan asked, putting his bottle down.

Donovan released a long-suffering sigh. "For you, yes. So spill your guts. Get it out."

Morgan glanced away for a moment and when he returned his gaze to Donovan he saw the questions lodged in the darkness of the eyes staring back at him. Knowing he couldn't waste any more time he said, "There are two reasons that I wanted to meet with you. The first is to let you know that I met with Edward Dunlap again."

Donovan nodded and lightly rubbed his chin, regarding his brother intently. "Does that mean you've finally made a decision about running for that city council at-large seat in the fall?" he asked his brother.

He'd known that for years a number of the African American leaders around town wanted Morgan to strongly consider a political career. He had charisma, charm and an ingrained sense of doing what was right. His community service—as well as his public service record—was astonishing and included such notable accomplishments as leading Charlotte's Economic Development and Planning Council.

Another plus was that Morgan had been born and raised in Charlotte. The Steeles were one of the first families to begin a black-owned business that now employed a lot of people and who didn't hesitate to pay their employees a very decent salary.

Another plus Donovan knew Morgan had in his cap was the Steele Corporation's infrastructure. They were a company that believed in being loyal to the people who worked for them. When they had a chance to make a bigger profit by outsourcing a lot of their production department, they had refused since it would have meant putting over five hundred people out of a job.

Yes, there was no doubt in Donovan's mind that if Morgan ever decided to seek a political office he would get it. Some even had him pegged as the man who would eventually become the city's first black mayor.

Only a selected number of individuals were born to be public servants, and he'd always felt that Morgan was one of them. And although Morgan downplayed such, Donovan knew that deep down Morgan did want to become a political candidate mainly because of his ingrained sense of always wanting to help people.

"No. I haven't made a decision, but I am giving it more thought than I did before. Dunlap feels the time is right. He's also afraid if I don't run, Roger Chadwick will, and both you and I know if that happens he will hurt the city more than help it."

Donovan chuckled harshly. "That's an understatement."

"I have to know that I have certain things in place before making my final decision, and one of them involves you," Morgan said.

"Me?"

"Yes. *You.* I'd like you to be my campaign manager if I do decide to run."

Donovan smiled proudly. That meant Morgan being a candidate was a high likelihood. "Consider it done."

Morgan nodded. "Thanks. Now for the other reason I wanted to meet with you. I met with Lena today because I've decided to sell my house and plan to buy a new one. She'll be handling both transactions for me."

Donovan looked at him and shook his head. "It's your house to do as you please with, but I'm surprised you'd want to sell it. You've always talked about how much you like your home. According to you it was the 'perfect' house."

"It still is, which is why I wanted to meet with you."

Donovan leaned back in his chair. The expression on his face was one indicating he was clearly confused. "Evidently, I'm missing some point here, so maybe you ought to go ahead and tell me what I got to do with you selling your house."

Morgan picked up his beer bottle and took another sip. "Lena mentioned that once I put my house on the market she'd probably begin showing it to a lot of people."

Donovan rolled his eyes toward the ceiling. "Yeah, that's usually how it works."

"That's all well and good," Morgan said, ignoring his brother's sarcasm. "But I don't want anybody to buy it."

"Then why in blazes are you selling it?"

Donovan waited for him to answer and when he saw Morgan wasn't quick with any answers, he couldn't help but laugh when he figured things out. "You're pretty damn desperate to resort to putting your house up for sale just to get on Lena's good side." Donovan's brows shot up. "But you still haven't told me what any of this has to do with me."

Morgan took another pull from his beer bottle. "I want Lena to try to sell it, but in the end I want to feel comfortable knowing the person buying it will take care of it."

"And?"

Morgan sighed. "And I want you to be the one to buy it."

First a grin spread across Donovan's face as he thought Morgan was joking. But after studying his brother's features and seeing Morgan was dead serious, Donovan began shaking his head adamantly. "No can do, man. I don't need a place as large as your house. My condo is just fine."

"But don't you want your space?"

Donovan took another swallow of his drink and said, "I have enough space, thank you very much. I do one woman at a time, so that's all the space I need. Besides, your house is on an acre of land. I don't do yards. I never got along with grass. I don't own a mower and don't plan to buy one. It doesn't bother me to pay those exceedingly high association fees for the golf course in my backyard, although I'm not a golfer. It goes with my image, one I want to keep. Besides, I always thought your place was too big for one person. I still do."

"I need you to buy it, Don."

"Aw, hell, Morgan, why me?"

"Because Chance, Bas and Vanessa already have homes, and Taylor and Cheyenne never stay in one place long enough to own anything but the clothes on their backs. You're my only hope."

"But I don't understand. If you like your house, why are you selling it in the first place? You never did answer that question, although I have an idea."

For a moment Morgan didn't say anything. Then he said, "And your idea is probably right. Selling my house is part of my current plan and that's all you need to know. I'm really hoping things don't get that far, that Lena will realize my present home is the perfect one for us. But just in case things don't go the way I want, I need to have a backup and I want you to be it."

Donovan leaned back in his seat and released a long sigh, the second one in a matter of less than thirty minutes. He studied his brother, the one known to want the perfect everything. Three years ago he had built what he'd touted as the perfect house, and now he was willing to risk losing it for what Morgan saw as the perfect woman. Go figure.

"Is she worth all this, Morgan?" Donovan asked, truly needing to know.

Morgan didn't say anything for a moment. It wasn't that Donovan's question had him thinking, it was just that he didn't know what he could say to make his brother understand. But he believed that although Donovan didn't have a clue how it felt to be undeniably drawn to one woman, one day he would. But for now the only thing he could do was answer the question as truthfully as he could.

"Yes, Donovan, Lena Spears is definitely worth it."

Chapter 2

After glancing around the room for the second time, Lena finally looked over at Morgan. "How can you even think of selling this place? Your home is simply beautiful."

Morgan smiled, pleased with her compliment. Her question was similar to the one Donovan had asked him last week, but of course he couldn't provide her with the same answer. However, it sent a jolt through his stomach that she liked his home. He'd been hoping she would. "I've outgrown the place and would like something bigger, more elegant. Your job is to find me something more perfect than what I already have."

He watched as she scanned the room again. It was just the living room. She hadn't seen the rest of the house, and he couldn't wait until she did. More than one person had offered to buy his home on the spot after seeing it, yet he had never once considered selling…until now, and only as a last resort. A part of him was still holding out that Lena would love it and want to live in it with him. But if she preferred living some place else, then he would gladly move.

"I'd like to know how you can outgrow something like this," she said, reclaiming his thought. "In my line of business I've been through plenty of homes, but none ever took my breath away from the moment I walked through the front door like this one did. There's no way this place won't sell quickly."

Her last statement was something he didn't want to hear, which was the main reason he'd gotten Donovan involved. "Come on and let me show you the rest of it."

An hour later he and Lena were sitting in his kitchen sipping glasses of iced tea. He tried not to make a big deal that technically this was the first drink they'd shared together alone. They had shared a drink that night at the charity ball, a glass of punch, while standing near the buffet table. And then at Chance and Kylie's wedding they had stood next to each other drinking champagne. The same thing had occurred at Bas and Jocelyn's wedding. But now he had her alone on his turf, and as he sat across from her watching her take slow sips of her tea, he couldn't help noticing how her eyes seemed to take on a darker shade in the March sunlight. Seeing her eye color change did things to his insides. And then there was her scent, a luscious fragrance that nearly had him groaning.

"I know you get tired of hearing me say this, Morgan, but your home is gorgeous," she said, breaking into his thoughts. "I'll be able to find a buyer with no problem, but to be honest with you I'm not sure I'll find a place better for you to live. It's just something about your home, the way you have it decorated, the layout. Even the yard is huge and just take a look at this kitchen." She glanced around. "It's a cook's dream. Any woman would love to lose herself in here. How long have you lived here?"

He pulled his gaze away from her mouth. He'd been watching every word flow from it while thinking of a million things he'd love to do with it, and every one of them was increasing the rate of his pulse. "For about three years now. I bought the land six years ago but didn't get around to building the house until then."

He decided not to go into details that it had taken him three years from the time he had purchased the land to finally approve a design from the architect he'd hired. In his book everything had to be perfect. His brothers would often tease him about always wanting things just right, to the point that it would drive them crazy at times, but he always ignored their taunts. He couldn't help that he was a stickler for how he wanted certain things he deemed important.

"I might as well tell you that Donovan might be interested in buying this place," he said, deciding now was as good a time as any to make that part known. He watched her arched brow rise in surprise.

"He is?"

"Yes, but I don't want you to concentrate on him as a potential buyer just yet. Show it to others, see what they think and how much they're willing to pay before I seriously consider Donovan's offer. I promised him first dibs, but I want to be sure if I do I'm offering him a fair price."

She nodded. "That sounds reasonable," she said, glancing down at her watch.

Morgan noticed the gesture. "Do you have another appointment this afternoon?" he asked, knowing she didn't. She had told him earlier that he was the last person she was scheduled to see that day, other than the lunch she had planned with Kylie around one.

She glanced up and met his eyes. "No, sorry if I appeared distracted for a moment but I was thinking of my mother. She went on a field trip with her adult day care today and usually I would have heard from them by now letting me know that she didn't fare well. With no phone call I'm hoping that means she had a good time."

He nodded. "Where did they go?"

"The zoo. How was your trip out of town?"

Sensing her need to change the subject he said, "It was great. I had a business meeting with a friend named Cameron Cody. I believe you met him at both Chance's and Bas's weddings."

She nodded as she took another sip of tea. "That's the guy who tried to take over your company at one time, right?"

Morgan chuckled, which he did every time he was reminded of that. "Yes, he's the one. In the end Cameron wasn't successful in doing that, but he was in forging a friendship with all of us…at least everyone except Vanessa. She never got over it."

"But you and your brothers did?"

"Yes. We couldn't help but respect a man like Cameron, a self-made millionaire. Although he was determined to add the Steele Corporation to his list of acquisitions, he wasn't ruthless about it. He's a sharp businessman, and the four of us couldn't help but admire him for it. After it was all over we all became good friends."

"I get the feeling Vanessa doesn't care for him much."

Morgan smiled. "No, she doesn't." He decided not to mention that after spending time with Cameron in Atlanta this weekend it seemed they had the same intentions regarding finally taking matters into their own hands to start relentlessly pursuing the women they wanted.

"I'd better be going. I don't want to take up too much more of your time," Lena said, coming to her feet.

It was on the tip of his tongue to try his luck and ask her out again, but he knew like all the other times chances were she would turn him down. Besides, the key to his plan being a success was getting her to assume he was no longer interested in her.

"You're not taking up any of my time unnecessarily. I like this place and want to make sure whoever buys it is worthy."

He stood and then asked, "So what's the next procedure?" He watched as she opened her folder.

"As far as this house goes, it's as good as sold. It has too many strong points for it not to be a quick buy. All the expensive moldings, the marble in the bathrooms and the bathrooms period. They're beautiful and spacious and you're using all the cabinet space to the best advantage. This house is rather large for one person. You're evidently someone who likes his space."

He shrugged. "Not really. I don't mind sharing my space with the right person."

"Well, to answer your question," Lena replied, "what's next is the installation of a lockbox. You don't have a problem with me showing your home when you're not here, do you?"

He wasn't crazy about the idea but knew he couldn't tell her that. "No, I don't have a problem with it."

"Good. I'll try to call before I drop by with anyone."

"That's fine. Do whatever you need to do." He came around the table to stand in front of her. "I'll walk you out since I need to leave myself. I have to drop back by the office to finish up some paperwork and then I'm expected to show up for dinner later at Bas and Jocelyn's place."

Lena smiled as she stood. "I can't help but smile every time I think of how Bas talked Jocelyn in changing their wedding date from June to February."

Morgan grinned. "Chase did the same thing with Kylie. Both Jocelyn and Kylie got cheated out of June weddings because of my eager brothers. I'm glad Jocelyn was able to finalize everything she had to do so she could move from Newton Grove to here permanently. Otherwise, we would have been tempted to ask Bas to take another leave of absence or he would have driven us all nuts."

"They seem so happy."

"They are, and so are Chance and Kylie. Marriage seems to agree with some people."

"Well, yes, I'm sure it does."

He watched how she quickly gathered up her belongings. He got the distinct impression that his closeness was bothering her. "I better get going," she said.

"Okay, I'll see you out."

As he walked her to the door he said, "I'd like weekly updates. Will that be a problem?"

She glanced over at him. "No, that won't be a problem. I'm checking on an area of homes a few miles from here. It's a new subdivision but I don't think the property is more than what you have now. You like a lot of land, don't you?"

"Yes, more yard for my children to play."

He could feel her gaze on him. "You want children?"

"Sure, one day. Don't you?"

"Yes, but…"

He turned to her when they reached the door. "But what?"

"Umm, but nothing. I'll see you later, Morgan," she said, offering him her hand for a business handshake. "And I appreciate you allowing me to handle things for you."

He glanced at her hand before taking it. "Like I said, you come highly recommended. One thing you'll discover about me, Lena, is that I choose my business associates carefully." *As carefully as I choose my lovers,* he decided not to add.

He saw the expression on her face the moment their hands touched. He also felt her response. Although she might wish otherwise, the chemistry between them was still there. He was tempted to lean in and kiss her. Take her mouth the way he'd thought of doing so many times. Once he slipped his tongue between her parted lips, there would be no stopping him. A kiss could be defined as friendly or intimate. Any kiss they shared would definitely be intimate.

The moment he released her hand she turned and he watched as she quickly began strolling down the brick walkway to her car, liking the sway of her hips as she did so. Today she was wearing another powerhouse business suit. This one was a mint green and brought out the rich brown coloring of her skin tone. Something else it brought out was the primal male inside him when he'd gotten close enough to notice she was also wearing a mint-green bra, which made him wonder what else under her clothes was the same color.

He sighed deeply as she pulled back out of his driveway. Part of his plan was to take things slow so she could get to know him, but all he could think about while sitting across from her at that table was speeding things up a bit, saying the hell with slow and taking her into his bedroom and making love to her like there was no tomorrow.

But he knew doing such a thing would only

result in a satisfaction of overstimulated hormones and he wanted something a lot more out of a relationship with Lena. So for now the between-the-sheets fantasies had to take a backseat to what was really important, even if the waiting killed him, because everything he was doing now would be all worth it in the end.

Lena let out a deep breath as soon as Morgan's home was no longer in sight. Talk about temptation, she thought, coming to a stop at a traffic light and pursing her lips. Each time her gaze had met his she had been tempted to reach across the table and trace her fingers across those delectable lips of his. That would have given her only a little contentment. What would really have satisfied the woman in her was to have plastered her mouth to his and kissed him the way she often thought of doing.

But that wasn't all. She could vividly recall when he had shown her his bedroom. The moment she had seen the king-size bed with royal-blue satin sheets, an all-consuming need had spread all through her body. And when he had left her side to show how the remote to his window blinds worked, her gaze had devoured him, appreciating how his lean and firm thighs fit his designer trousers and how his broad, muscled shoulders fit the white shirt he wore. And just for a moment, when he had leaned across the bed to brush a piece of lint off the bedspread, she had imagined herself in that bed, tangled in those sheets with him. By the time she had taken a gulp of that ice-cold tea he'd prepared, she had needed it to cool off.

Inwardly she groaned when the traffic light turned green. She had to let go of this obsession since it would lead nowhere. She glanced at her watch again. She and Kylie had their regular lunch date, and today they would plan for Kylie's baby shower.

She smiled thinking that her friend was having another baby after almost fifteen years. But this time the pregnancy would be totally different. Kylie was not that sixteen-year-old who had found herself facing a teenage pregnancy alone after her parents had turned their backs on her. Now she was a woman married to a wonderful man who loved her and who would make her baby a wonderful father.

Lena couldn't help but be happy for her best friend, and inwardly she could admit she was a little envious although such happiness could not have happened to a more deserving person than Kylie. But still, that didn't stop Lena's heart from aching from what she didn't have. Here she was, at thirty-one still the bridesmaid but never the bride, still the godmother but never the mother. And what was so sad was knowing she would never be a bride or a mother.

She inhaled deeply, refusing to give the state of her future any more thought that day.

"What's this I hear about you selling your home, Morgan?"

Morgan lifted a brow. He highly suspected that Bas had heard the news from Donovan, not that it was a secret.

"Yes, you heard right," he said, accepting the glass of wine his brother was offering him.

"How come?"

Morgan gave a sigh of relief. At least Donovan hadn't told Bas everything. "What do you mean how come?"

"Just what I ask," Bas said, dropping into the lounge chair across from where Morgan sat. "How come? You love that house. As you've told us so many times, it's perfect for you."

Jocelyn was in the kitchen and Morgan could only hope she wasn't privy to their conversation. "Things change."

"Bullshit. Tell that to someone else. Things might change but you don't. You've had this obsession with things being ideal in your life for as long as I can remember. So what's really going on with you, Morgan? What's the real reason you're selling your house? Discovered you're sitting on a gold mine or something?"

"Wished it was that simple," Morgan managed to say finally, studying his glass of wine for a moment before lifting his gaze to Bas's curious one. "Colin Powell once said, and I quote, 'There are no secrets to success. It is the result of preparation, hard work and learning from failure.'"

Bas rolled his eyes. "Will you give it to me straight, Morgan?"

Morgan smiled as he momentarily traced his finger around the rim of his glass. Bas was a troubleshooter; he looked for problems where there weren't any. Morgan glanced back up and met his brother's gaze. "Okay, Bas, you want me to give it to you straight? Then here goes. Lena Spears."

Morgan watched his brother's expression. For a moment he looked genuinely bewildered. Then slowly, Morgan saw the exact moment he figured things out. For a while there Morgan had gotten worried since Bas wasn't normally a slow man.

"I hope you know what you're doing," Bas said sharply, narrowing his eyes at him.

"Trust me, I do. I want her, Bas."

"Tell me something I don't know, Morgan. That's been evident now for over a year. It's also been evident to everyone but you, it seems, that she doesn't want to be wanted…at least not by you."

"Then it's up to me to convince her otherwise."

"And you'll go so far as to sell your house to do it?"

"Whatever it takes. Wish me luck."

Bas shook his head, smiling. "You need more than luck, brother. You need prayer. I get the distinct impression that Lena likes her life just the way it is."

"I got that impression too, and I wanted to know why such a beautiful woman would not want a man in it."

"Did you ask Kylie?"

"Yes."

"And what did she say?"

"At first she was tight-lipped, like she didn't want to betray Lena's confidences or something. Then she mumbled something about the men in Lena's past not being able to get past the fact that she and her mother are a package deal."

Bas frowned. "If that's true, then those weren't men, they were assholes who must have been hatched. Who in their right mind would even think about making a person choose between a lover and a parent?"

"How about someone like Dr. Derek Peterson?"

Bas's frown deepened. "He's a good example that what I said is true since everyone knows he's an asshole."

Morgan chuckled. Derek, who'd always taken ego trips even while in high school, was not a favorite of the Steele Brothers since that night a few years ago when he'd tried pulling his aggressive macho ways on Vanessa. Ignoring their advice she had gone out with him. The date had ended rather quickly when she had to resort to kneeing him in the groin when he proved he didn't know the meaning of the word *no*. He never forgave Vanessa for using that technique on him, and to this day was still pissed at the Steele brothers for having taught her how to use it.

"Well, he must not have been the only one for Lena to have developed a complex about it to the point where she thinks the majority of men think that way. I intend to prove otherwise, and certain things can't be rushed. Using her as my Realtor will buy me some time."

He took a sip of his wine, determined to make Bas understand as he'd done Donovan a few days ago. "I'm serious when I said I want her, Bas. But more importantly," he said, meeting his brother's gaze, "I intend to have her."

"So, Mom, how was the trip to the zoo?"

"It was nice. Mr. Bannister got sick again and Ms. Lilly wanted Mr. Arnold to share his wheelchair but he wouldn't."

Lena nodded. She knew Ms. Lilly was an older woman in her early eighties who had begun showing signs of Alzheimer's last year. On several occasions she had assumed Odessa Spears was her daughter and would try to make her follow her commands. "What about Ms. Emily? How did she do today?" she asked, and glanced over and watched her mother smile.

"Why, Emily did just fine with this being her first trip and all. But she had company. Her granddaughter and great-granddaughter went with us as chaperones. Did I ever tell you that she had six grands and two great-grands?"

Lena's stomach tightened since she knew where this conversation was headed. "Yes, Mama, you told me."

"And Emily agrees with me that it's a shame that I don't even have a grand. She said she can't believe a young woman as pretty as you can't find herself a man."

Lena sighed deeply. There was no way she could tell her mother that men were out there a dime a dozen and she didn't have to "find" one. The problem was hooking up with one who didn't have stipulations that weren't acceptable to her. Lena knew her mother's heart would be crushed if she ever discovered the real reason men didn't come calling and those who did usually stopped real quick, as if in a hurry once they discovered her role in her mother's life.

"Mom, like I told you, my job keeps me busy."

"No job should keep a woman too busy for a man. You're thirty-one. I was married to your father before my twenty-first birthday and we were so happy together. That man was my life. You came along twenty years later and then the both of you became my life. A woman couldn't have been happier. A husband and a child have a way of fulfilling a woman's life."

"I'm sure that's true, Mom, but—"

"And take a look at Kylie. I love Tiffany dearly with her being your godchild and all, but a new baby is nice and it didn't take Kylie long after her marriage to do her duty."

Lena shook her head. *Her duty.* She didn't want to think about what her mother figured her duty was.

"But I don't want to talk about Kylie. You're my daughter and I want to talk about you."

Lena sighed. Her mother hadn't been this talkative in a long time. A part of her was happy about it, but she would be even happier if they discussed another subject. "Mom, we've talked before. They don't make men like they used to," she said, coming to a stop at a traffic light.

She glanced over at her mom and met her gaze when Odessa asked, "Is that what's bothering you? Are you figuring there isn't a man out there like your daddy was? Probably not, but it's the woman who usually makes the marriage and not the man. You just have to let him think that he does. Why, I can recall when your father…"

Lena pulled off when the traffic light changed to green as her mother relived pleasant memories. She was grateful for the change in subjects, because if they had stayed on their same conversation path, there was no way she wouldn't eventually have lost it. Having lunch with Kylie and seeing how pregnant she looked made her unconsciously rub her stomach wishing more than anything a baby could be there.

She cleared her throat in an attempt to keep her tear ducts from working. For some reason she'd been in a melancholy mood lately, but she knew it would eventually pass and she would snap out of it.

Considering everything, she really didn't have much of a choice.

Chapter 3

Lena glanced around when she entered the restaurant. She had been on her way to the Steele Corporation for a meeting with Morgan when she received a call from her secretary saying Morgan wanted to meet with her here instead of his office.

She sighed, feeling tired from a restless night. Her mother had had another outburst for her father and it had taken a while to get her settled back down. It always pained Lena to watch her mother relive her grief. After taking her mother to the day care this morning she had stopped by to visit with Delphine Moore, her mother's social worker.

Delphine had explained that the reason her mother kept having her bouts of grief, even after six years, was that she hadn't yet found anything to fill the void in her life left by her father. God knows it hadn't been for lack of trying on Lena's part. According to both Delphine and Lena's mother's family physician, Odessa's issues, both mentally and physically, stemmed from the same thing. She needed something motivating in her life, something that would give her the will and desire to keep living.

Something like a grandchild.

The conversation she'd had with her mother a few days ago was still firmly embedded in Lena's mind. She knew her mother was lonely and that was understandable. She also knew her mother probably saw her life slowly drifting away without the love of a grandchild to cherish. A part of Lena wished more than anything she could give her mother a granddaughter or grandson to love during her remaining days on earth, but such a thing wasn't possible. Kylie had suggested that she try looking into programs where elderly adults could volunteer to act as surrogate grandparents. Since her mother got around fairly well with minimum help on her good days, that was one idea worth checking out. Lena's heart sank every time she thought of her mother being unhappy.

"May I help you, miss?"

The waiter's question reined Lena's thoughts back to the present. "Yes. I'm to meet Morgan Steele here."

The waiter smiled. "Yes, please follow me. Mr. Steele is waiting."

As she followed the waiter it wasn't long before she was staring into the contours of Morgan's handsome face when he stood for her approach. As usual he was dressed in a tailored suit and looked the epitome of a successful businessman. By the time she reached his table, her heart was jumping crazily in her chest. Although the eyes staring at her were intense, his facial expression was solid, unreadable. But that was all right, she tried assuring herself. If he were to look at her any other way, with even a hint of an open invitation right now, her Gemini twin would be tempted to come out, and heaven forbid if that happened. She had dreamed of Morgan last night, and those dreams were still vivid in her mind. Her body had been flooded with adrenaline of the most sensual kind.

In her fantasy he was an expert lover, and she would bet that in reality he would be the same.

By the time she reached his table, her heart was just about ready to explode in her chest. She cleared her throat. "Morgan," she said, automatically reaching her hand out to him.

He took it and for a moment she thought he held it a second longer than necessary. "Lena. Sorry about the change in plans but I'm glad you could meet me here. I appreciate your flexibility."

"No problem," she said, taking her seat with fluid ease. The place Morgan had chosen for lunch was elegant and the furnishings spoke the part. The chairs were soft leather with high-contoured backs for both comfort and style. There was a lit candle in the middle of the table, and it came to her attention for the first time that they were sitting in the back, almost in an alcove that provided a semblance of seclusion and a bit of intimacy—not at all in keeping which what should be a business meeting.

As if he read her thoughts he said, "I had a business meeting here earlier and decided that instead of going back to the office or changing location we could meet here. I hope you don't mind."

She shook her head. "No, I don't mind. It's a nice place."

"Yes, it is."

Morgan knew he couldn't tell her that this was the place he had intended to bring her for their first lunch date, which she never agreed to. And he'd had to do some underhanded maneuverings for her to be with him now. "So, I understand you have information for me," he said.

"Yes. I might have an interested party for your home as well as a place you want to look at. It's located not far in—"

"Well, aren't we a cozy twosome."

A sudden wave of irritation touched Morgan when he glanced up into the face of Cassandra Tisdale, a staunch member of Charlotte's elite social group. She was one of the most self-absorbed women he knew, and to top it off, she was Bas's former fiancée.

The only good thought about that was the word *former*. Bas had broken off the engagement the night of Chance and Kylie's wedding and hadn't given the family a reason why. But it hadn't been that hard to figure things out. Cassandra and Bas were as different as day and night, and a marriage would have made them the odd couple, whereas Bas and Jocelyn were a perfect match.

He slowly came to his feet. "Cassandra, I didn't

know you were back." Rumor had it that she left town for an extended trip to her parents' vacation home in the Bahamas a couple of weeks before Bas's wedding because she didn't want to be anywhere near Charlotte when the event took place.

"Oh yes, I returned this week. I had a wonderful time."

Doing nothing, he surmised. Cassandra saw her role in life as to not earn a living but to give parties, entertain and remain a social butterfly. She was wealthy and intended to marry wealthy. Rumor further had it that since her breakup with Bas she had set her sights on Donovan's best friend, Bronson. Luckily Bronson was smart enough to not give Cassandra the time of day.

Everyone also knew she had only latched on to Bas in the first place after Dane Bradford had gotten back with his wife, Sienna. Cassandra had been Dane's girlfriend in high school, but the two had broken up when they'd gone to separate colleges. When they returned to Charlotte she had figured Dane would come rushing back to her. Instead he met and married Vanessa's best friend, Sienna Davis.

Almost two years ago Dane and Sienna began having bad times in their marriage and filed for a divorce. Both Cassandra's family as well as Dane's had hoped with Sienna out of the picture Cassandra could become part of Dane's life again. That didn't happen because Dane and Sienna eventually got back together. Not long after that Cassandra had set her sights on Bas. Eventually, she and Bas had become engaged, but Bas had called off the wedding before a date could be set.

"Glad to hear you had a wonderful time." He glanced over at Lena. "I'm sure you know Lena."

Cassandra's smile didn't quite reach her eyes. "Yes, I know, Lena," she said, giving Lena only a cursory glance. "I'm really surprised to see the two of you here together in such a cozy setting. I'm disappointed in you, Morgan. I know you can do better."

He heard Lena's sharp intake of breath at the direct insult, and anger, to a degree he didn't think possible, took over him. "Just like I knew Bas could do better, and I was right. I hope you get the chance to meet Jocelyn. She's just what Bas needs, and the Steeles are proud to have her as a member of the family."

When she picked up the water glass, no doubt to throw the contents in his face, he said, "Be careful, Cassandra. Your spiteful claws are showing, and I thought you were too socially cultivated for that." He took his seat, not giving her the courtesy of remaining standing in her presence. "Now if you will excuse me I would like to get back to my lunch guest."

He heard her place the glass back on the table and when he was sure she had walked away, he glanced over at Lena. "I apologize for that."

Lena waved off his apology. "Don't. I've known a long time that I'm not Cassandra's favorite person, ever since I became friends with Sienna. I recommend her to decorate a lot of the houses I sell. So Cassandra's insults don't bother me. She assumed we're here together for something else other than business and she was wrong…as usual."

She leaned closer over the table. "Now, what I was saying before we were interrupted, Morgan, is that I think I've found an interested buyer for your home as well as a place you might like to purchase. I didn't put a contract on your place because of what you told me about Donovan, but I can tell you they are willing to make you a good offer for it."

He nodded, inwardly not caring what kind of offer they made. "Who are they?"

"The Edwardses. He's an executive for Brook-shire Industries and his job is transferring him here. Matthew and his wife, Joan, are in their thirties and they have three kids. Meghan is ten, Matt Junior is eight. Then there's Sarah. She's five and is handicapped and confined to a wheelchair, but somehow she can swim with assistance. I think she's the one who liked your pool the best. When she saw it she—"

"You showed them the house already?" he asked in surprise.

Lena raised a brow, wondering what kind of question that was. "Of course I showed them the house. You did give me permission to show your home while you weren't there, didn't you?"

He sighed deeply. "Of course." And being the top-notch Realtor that she was, she wasn't wasting any time doing what she thought he wanted her to do. "What about this place you want me to see?"

She smiled. "I think you're going to like it. In fact I think you're going to like it even better than what you have now, it's just that beautiful."

He lifted a brow. She had piqued his interest if she thought such a thing. "Just where is this place?"

He could see the excitement in her eyes when she said, "It's just minutes from the airport, which will help with your travels, and in some areas it backs up against Lake Wylie, if you're interested in waterfront property."

He nodded. He hadn't been before, but he could be if she was. "So, when can I take a look at it?"

"Whenever you're free."

"Okay, how about today, after lunch?"

Lena blinked. She hadn't expected that. "Lunch?"

"Yes. Since you're here you might as well join me for lunch, unless you've eaten already or have made other plans."

"No, but didn't you eat lunch during your earlier business meeting here?" she inquired curiously.

He lifted impeccably clad shoulders with a negative shake of his head. "No. Anthony and I shared drinks, not a meal. I haven't eaten since breakfast and I need something. If you'd rather we not go check out this place today we can do it at another time. Just call my secretary and see when she'll be able to work you into my calendar again later this week."

Lena didn't like the sound of that. She knew how busy Morgan was and decided she needed to show him the place as soon as she could. "No, it's okay. If today is better for you, then it's fine with me. No, I haven't eaten anything and don't have plans. I can stay and join you for lunch."

He smiled. "Good." He glanced around and called a waiter over to their table.

"Yes, Mr. Steele?"

"Ms. Spears will be joining me for lunch, Ricardo. May we have two menus?"

"Certainly, sir."

When the waiter walked off, Lena said, "I take it that you come here often."

"Yes, I usually hold my business meetings here."

"Oh."

Raising his glass he took a sip of his wine, knowing with those words he had effectively removed any thoughts from Lena's mind that his invitation for her to join him for lunch was anything other than business.

Lena glanced over at Morgan as he expertly maneuvered his SUV toward their destination, which was a twenty-minute drive from the restaurant. He had suggested saving time by using one vehicle, preferably his. That way she was free to cover the amenities the place had to offer while he did the driving.

In some faraway recess of her mind, she knew it was time to begin going over those things with him, but for some reason she welcomed the quietness between them and wasn't ready for conversation of any kind to intrude. Besides, he seemed to be in his own world, his gaze fixed on the stretch of road in front of him. Nothing played, not even his radio, and she felt a tinge of uneasiness at the thought he could possibly hear her breathing, an erratic sound of wanting and need that she was trying hard to hide. But around him it was nearly impossible.

Even now the scent of him, definitely male, infiltrated her nostrils, sent heat coursing through her blood. In the past she could control her urges and her desires just by turning her mind and thoughts off to them. But since meeting Morgan, she found such a thing difficult, almost impossible, especially when they were in close proximity to each other.

She'd been conscious of a slow, nagging ache in the lower part of her body ever since he had walked her out of the restaurant to his vehicle. By the time she had gotten seated in his truck she'd been almost breathless. And when he had casually bent over her to snap her seat belt in place, it took everything she had to force her Gemini twin back from taunting him by pushing her cleavage forward, showing him as much of her breasts as she could beneath the droopy neckline of her blouse, and go even further by grabbing his tie and pulling him in closer; to have her mouth and tongue ready, willing and wet to meet his and—

"Okay, what you got for me?"

His question snapped her out of her daytime fantasy and she glanced over at him and met his gaze. It was on the tip of her tongue to respond that what she had for him was anything he wanted and it didn't have to be within reason. He had brought the car to a stop at a traffic light and was staring over at her beneath thick, long lashes. That ache in the lower part of her body intensified.

More than ever today she was aware of the absence of her panty hose. Usually, she wore a business suit, but because it was one of those rare warm days in March, she had decided to wear a knee-length melon-striped poplin skirt with a melon-colored pullover droopy-neck tunic sweater that flowed past her waist and a pair of flats.

She reached down by her leg to retrieve her leather portfolio to pull out the papers she needed and said, "Ashton Oaks is one of the premier neighborhoods of the Palisades that contain a limited edition of custom homes within a beautiful gated enclave and is in close proximity to the Palisades Country Club."

Morgan nodded. He was aware of the Palisades

because of the magnificent golf course that bordered it. "What's the price range of the homes?" he asked.

"Between seven hundred and two million. The one I'm going to show you falls in between, and I think when you see it you will agree that it's going to exceed your wildest dreams with its custom kitchens, fantasy bathrooms, glorious—"

"Fantasy bathrooms?" Morgan couldn't resist interrupting to ask, while raising a brow.

Lena chuckled. "Yes. You'll know what I mean when you see it. And because over three hundred acres of the land is set aside to preserve nature, there are plenty of hiking and equestrian trails."

"Sounds like a real nice place."

She smiled over at him after closing her folder. "I think you're going to be pleased. It's the ultimate in prestigious living. I really don't think you're going to find anything better."

He brought his SUV to a halt at a stop sign and glanced over at her, appreciating how the fabric of her sweater clung to her full breasts and how the rich coloring of her honey-brown hair fell in lustrous curls past her shoulders. It was his opinion that she had a mouth that was begging to be kissed, and he decided right then and there that she was wrong. He would find something better than the place she was taking him, and that was the place he intended to one day be, which was in her arms, in her bed, inside her body.

"The turnoff is up ahead, Morgan."

Morgan was convinced he wasn't imagining things when he heard that breathless catch in her voice. "All right." He tried putting all his concentration on his driving but found he couldn't. Even now his every breath was filled with the succulent scent of her as it floated through the confines of his vehicle. He decided to get control back before he blew things by pulling the truck to the side of the road and kissing the living daylights out of her.

"You mentioned one of the Edwards children was handicapped. What happened?"

"I didn't want to appear insensitive by asking. I think possibly a birth defect but I'm not sure. But Sarah is the cutest thing, simply adorable. She was ready to get into your pool that day."

Morgan chuckled. "Was she? She sounds like Tiffany the first time she saw it," he said of the niece he'd inherited after his brother's marriage to Kylie. He knew Tiffany was also Lena's godchild. His face formed in a thoughtful expression when he recalled how Chance's son, Marcus, along with

Tiffany, had managed to get their parents together. Too bad there was no one out there looking out for him and Lena.

"Turn right at the next corner, please, and stop. I'll get us passage through the gates."

Moments later Morgan brought his car to a stop at the gated entryway, and after Lena had talked to the guard to gain clearance, they were driving through. His breath actually caught at the impossibly beautiful homes he saw showcased, all custom designed and reflecting varying architectural styles. He immediately concluded that this was one extraordinary neighborhood from the lush landscaping to the pristine creeks that ran along the back properties of some.

"Pull into the next driveway on your left."

He did and he had to stop the moment his vehicle pulled into the yard. Before him sat what had to be the most regal and provincial home he'd ever seen. Completely brick, the three-story structure was twice the size of his present home, definitely a lot for one man. But then, he didn't intend to live in it alone. He would have a wife, a number of children and a mother-in-law whom he would gladly welcome with open arms.

"So what do you think?"

He turned to Lena when she asked the question. He smiled. "Umm, I'm curious to know what you think."

He watched as her mouth pursed. "I think this place has your name on it."

He chuckled, deciding not to tell her that if his name was on it, then her name was on it as well.

Chapter 4

So this was a fantasy bathroom, Morgan surmised as he studied the huge room that contained a Roman spa with trompe l'oeil walls, the Portuguese cork floors, the romantic recessed lightings, the cornice tile moldings that framed the wall mirror and the chrome fixtures. And then he couldn't omit the stone fireplace, the first he'd ever seen placed in a bathroom where you could soak away a day's worth of stress while enjoying the view of a blazing flame.

The house contained four other bathrooms and

they were just as elegant. The walls behind the bathtubs displayed a convergence of ceramic-tile styles against a backdrop of decorative squares and mosaic insets that appeared hand-carved.

But the elegance didn't stop there. The master suite connected to the main house by a glass breezeway with elevator access. There was also an in-law suite on the first floor that was the size of a small apartment. The massive great room with its thirty-foot ceilings and eight-foot-wide brick fireplace added an expressive intricate touch, and the huge kitchen with its granite-top island and ceramic tile floors did more than add a finishing touch. They provided enhancements not normally found in most custom homes, including the one he was living in now.

He turned and leaned against a kitchen counter. Although when he'd made the request he hadn't thought it was possible, Lena had done just what he had asked her to do. She had found a home more perfect than the one he now owned. "I really like this house, Lena," he said quite honestly. "Not only is it a home but it's also a private retreat."

He watched the smile that appeared on her face. "I like it, too, and hoped that you would. I have others to show you but I thought this one was yours."

Morgan shook his head. It definitely was his…and hers. "So what's next?" he asked.

"I prefer you not put a binder on it yet. I feel confident that I can work with the developer to get a few more amenities. I'm not saying he will give us any, but it's worth a try, and I wouldn't be doing my job as your Realtor if I didn't get you the best bang for your buck."

He swallowed and wished she hadn't said the word *bang*. At the moment he would gladly take the best bang for his buck. Even now with her standing across the room he couldn't help but notice her bare legs and would do anything to get up close and personal just to run his hands up her voluptuous thighs. After getting a glimpse of her yellow bra that day he wondered if she always matched her underthings with her outerwear. He would love to investigate, to check things out for himself by going up under her skirt to see just what was beneath it.

She glanced down at her watch. "Oops, I need to leave. I almost forgot I need to pick my mother up a little early today since they're having a meeting at the center. I'll barely have time to make it once you take me back to the restaurant to pick up my car."

"Then I won't. I'll just take you straight to the place to get your mother."

She shook her head. "You don't have to do that, really."

"I'm sure I don't but I don't mind. Besides, I'd like to meet your mother."

She lifted a brow. "Why?"

"Because I've heard a lot about her."

A bemused look touched Lena's features. "You have?"

"Yes."

"From who?"

"Kylie, Tiffany. She wasn't able to make it to Kylie's wedding. I understand she was under the weather."

Lena nodded knowing it was a lot more than that. "It just so happened that Chance and Kylie got married on what would have been my parents' fiftieth wedding anniversary had my father lived. They'd already been married twenty years before I was born."

"Wow, I didn't know that. I'm sure losing your father was hard on her."

Lena nodded. "Yes, it was. They had a rather close relationship, and although he's been gone for six years now, she still has some rough times. The holidays are extremely hard, especially Christmas since it was the day they married. And of course his birthday, which happens to be on the Fourth of July. She goes into a state of depression every year around those days."

Morgan nodded as he thought of his own parents. They would be celebrating their fortieth wedding anniversary in a few years. They, too, had a close relationship and he knew if anything were to happen to either parent, the remaining one would have a difficult time adjusting as well.

At that moment he felt an astounding respect and admiration for Lena. She had technically placed her social life on hold to take care of her mother. He and his bothers had unanimously decided when and if the time came not to place their parents in a nursing home if it was reasonably possible not to do so. Like Lena, they would become their parents' primary caretakers.

When he saw her glance down at her watch again, he said, "Come on. I want to make sure you're there to pick up your mother on time."

It was on the tip of Lena's tongue to tell him that she preferred that he not go. She could just imagine what her mother would think if a man accompanied her to pick her up as it had been over three years since she was actually out on a date. The last guy she'd dated had been Dr. Derek Peterson, who'd had the nerve to tell her that they could pick up their relationship once she put her mother in her own place and stop spending so much time with her. She was glad she hadn't gotten any further with him than the first kiss. After saying what he'd said the man had really turned her stomach.

Once they were back in Morgan's SUV her lips quivered slightly with nerves. Maybe she needed to prepare Morgan in case her mother did something crazy like bring up the subject of grandbabies, her favorite subject lately. "Morgan?"

He glanced over at her as he backed the vehicle out of the driveway. "Yes?"

"My mother. I think I need to prepare you about something so you won't be surprised, in case she brings it up."

"Okay, what is it?"

"She wants grandkids."

"Oh, I see."

Even as he said the words, Lena doubted if he really saw at all and decided to explain. "She's getting older and—"

"Lena, you don't have to explain. I have parents, too, remember. And when it comes to wanting grandkids they're just as bad."

"They are?"

"Yes. For years Marcus was enough for them, but then they started throwing out hints to the four of us again. They felt Chance needed to remarry and Bas, Donovan and I needed to find wives. Now with Bas married and Chance with a new baby on the way, they're satisfied for now, but I'm not counting on it lasting too long. They'll be looking at me and Donovan again in a few years."

A few moments later he asked, "What about you, Lena?"

She lifted a brow. "What about me?"

"I asked you before and you said you wanted kids…but. You never explained what that *but* meant."

Lena recalled that day a couple of weeks ago. She met his gaze when he halted at a stop sign. "*But* means that I would love to have children of my own one day and I would love for my children to know my mother while she's still here with me in good health and a good frame of mind. But since I'm not married and don't see myself getting married in my near or distant future, then it doesn't matter how much I love kids or want them, does it?"

Yes it did. Morgan's jaw tightened and he wished to earth that he could tell her right then and there that it did matter because he was willing to give her as many babies as she wanted. He could provide their child a loving, stable environment that included two parents and grandparents. And he didn't have a problem with Lena being her mother's primary caretaker. They would do it together, share the responsibility. And he would be able to provide all the financial security she'd ever want.

But at the moment he was too deep into his plan of pursuit to tell her that. He would have to show her better than to tell her. In the past men had disappointed her in such a way that it would be hard for Lena to put her complete trust in one again. So he would take his time and continue with his plan to build her trust and belief that he was different. He had to prove that all the other men in her life had been Mr. Wrong but he was her Mr. Right.

When he brought the car to the gate to exit out of the subdivision he smiled and said, "Don't worry. Your mother and I will get along great."

Lena inwardly sighed. That was exactly what she was afraid of. And then when Morgan stopped coming around the way the others had once they realized that her mother was a permanent fixture in her life, she wondered just what her mother was going to think.

* * *

"Who are you, young man?"

Before Morgan could respond Lena quickly answered as she snapped her mother's seat belt in place. "Mom, this is a client of mine, Morgan Steele. I was out showing him a house and time slipped away. He was kind enough to offer to bring me here to pick you up."

"Oh." Odessa, who was sitting in the front passenger seat, smiled over at Morgan, in the driver's seat. "That was nice of you, Mr. Steele." She then bunched her brows. "I know another Steele. Kylie's husband."

Morgan smiled. "That's Chance, my brother."

The woman's face crinkled into an even wider smile. "So, you're one of those Steele boys."

Morgan chuckled. He hadn't heard him and his brothers referred to that way in a long time. "Yes, ma'am, I am."

"I heard there were four of you."

"Yes, there are."

"Another one got married recently, right?"

"Yes, that was my brother Sebastian."

"You and your other brother are still single?"

"Mom! Please don't make Morgan feel like he's part of an inquisition," Lena said from the backseat as Morgan drove away from the adult day care center.

Odessa glanced over at Morgan. "Sorry about that, son."

He chuckled again. "No harm's been done, Ms. Spears. And to answer your question, yes, my brother Donovan and I are still single."

To avoid her mother asking Morgan any questions about his personal life, Lena quickly asked her how things had gone at the center today. Odessa then went into a lengthy explanation, filling everyone in on the happenings of that day. Lena sat in the backseat thinking most of it was an everyday occurrence, especially the information about Mr. Talbot trying to eat Ms. Meriwether's lunch. But what was different today was that her mother had another set of ears, attentive ears. Lena knew Morgan was just being nice but he was hanging on to her mother's every word; and the more he hung on, the more her mother had to say. She couldn't recall the last time her mother was so chatty with a stranger.

From her position in the backseat Lena watched Morgan. Although he kept his eyes focused on the road, he was still attuned to what her mother was saying and would make occasional comments. Lena finally decided to tune out the conversation and focus on him.

The man had a very sexy mouth. That was one of the first things she had noticed about him the first night they met, which was probably the reason she kept having those fantasies of kissing it. Then there were his hands, the ones that were now gripping the steering wheel. She could just imagine him gripping her thighs in just the same way, while his fingers inched upward toward that heated place and—

"Isn't that wonderful, Lena?"

She blinked, realizing her mother had spoken to her, had asked her a question. "Excuse me, Mom, what did you say? My thoughts were elsewhere."

"I said, isn't it wonderful that Morgan is coming to dinner on Sunday?"

"What!" Lena said, switching her gaze to Morgan and meeting his in the rearview mirror in wild confusion. What was her mother talking about? Morgan was not coming to dinner on Sunday.

"Did I miss something?" she asked, trying to ignore the intensity in the dark eyes staring back at her in the mirror.

"Your mother asked when the last time was that I had homemade chicken and dumplings, and I told her it's been a while. She was kind enough to invite me over on Sunday since she'll be cooking some then."

Lena snatched her gaze from Morgan to stare at the back of her mother's head. "When did you decide to cook?" She couldn't recall the last time her mother had been motivated to go into the kitchen to prepare dinner. Usually Lena did the cooking.

"When Morgan said it's been a while since he'd had chicken and dumplings. I think he should get a taste of mine at least once."

"That's kind of you, Mom, and I'm certain Morgan appreciates the invitation, but I'm sure he has other things to do on Sunday."

"No, I don't."

A surprised brow lifted as Lena met Morgan's gaze in the rearview mirror again. She'd been trying to help him out of what she thought was a situation he hadn't really wanted to be in. "You don't?"

He chuckled. "No, I don't."

"Then it's all settled," Odessa Spears was saying with a smile in her voice. "And I think I'm going to bake a peach cobbler as well. Do you like peach cobbler, Morgan?"

"Yes, ma'am."

"Good."

Kylie Steele smiled, seeing the look of grief on the face of the woman who'd been her best friend since high school. They were having their weekly lunch session at their favorite restaurant. "Come on, Lena. Morgan having dinner at your place can't be that bad."

Lena frowned. "That's what you think. You know that he asked me out a few times and I turned him down, and I had worked so hard making sure he understood there could never be anything between us but friendship. And with him being a client, I've been trying to keep things strictly business between us, and now thanks to Mom he might get the wrong idea and I don't want that."

Kylie took a sip of her apple juice, her eyes meeting Lena's over the rim of her glass. Once she set the glass down on the table she asked, "Okay, Lena. Tell me. What's going on here? What is it that you really want?"

Lena shrugged. "I don't know what you mean."

"No, I think that you do. This is Kylie, remember, the one person who knows you like a book. Pregnancy didn't destroy any of my brain cells. I know the reason you turned Morgan down all those times. You're convinced he's no different than the Derek Petersons of the world."

Lena shook her head. "I never said he was anything like Derek. But then, I have to be fair and objective in dealing with men, Kylie. Taking care of an elderly parent is a huge undertaking, but I do it with pleasure and love because it's *my* mom. I don't see it just as a responsibility, I see it as a way to gladly give back all those things she's given to me over the years."

She took a sip of her wine before continuing. "But I can't expect others to see it that way. Mom is seventy-one and not in the best of health. Morgan's parents are in their late fifties, still alive, and are able to do things together. I'm all Mom has and that's okay. I don't have time to devote to a serious relationship. Being with her takes up most of my time."

"But it doesn't have to be that way, Lena. Your mom is in good health so it's not like she needs a sitter around the clock and—"

"Where would a relationship lead, Kylie? I've never been one to get into casual affairs and maybe that's my downfall. If I could indulge in one, then things would be just great and I wouldn't hurt when the affair ended because I could just brush myself off and start on another. But I can't do that. I get involved with all my emotions."

"You really liked Derek, didn't you?" Kylie asked softly, remembering the man who'd once had the nerve to try and hit on her right in front of Lena. What a jerk!

Emotions, thick and painful, lodged in Lena's throat. "He was a real charmer, I have to admit. I'm just glad I never slept with him. Then him walking away like he did would really have been humiliating. But to answer your question, yes, I really liked him but I didn't love him. I would have begun falling in love with him if I hadn't started seeing his true side. He was just like a spoiled child. He wanted to make me choose between him and my mother and he was too stupid to see there wasn't a choice. But to give me an ultimatum like that showed just what kind of person he was."

"Yes, it did. But let's get back to Morgan for a moment. You can't tell me you don't like him just a little."

Lena couldn't help but smile. "What's there not to like? He's good-looking, has good manners, he's a successful businessman. When I quoted him the price of that house I showed him a couple of days ago, he didn't bat an eye."

"But?"

"But even if I didn't have Mom I still wouldn't get involved with him. I'm way out of my league with him. I can see him with a totally different woman by his side, and I can't risk losing my heart to him. It's as simple as that."

She studied the contents of her glass for a moment, then said, "I didn't tell you that Morgan and I ran into Cassandra Tisdale the day we had our business meeting at that restaurant in town."

Kylie raised a brow. "Cassandra Tisdale? She's back?"

"Yes, and her fangs are sharper than ever. She made a very rude comment about Morgan and me being together."

Kylie frowned. "What kind of comment?"

"Something about how he could do better."

Kylie leaned back in her chair with a look of incredulity on her face. "I can't believe the nerve of that woman," she said, remembering the first time she had come into contact with Cassandra. "For someone who's supposed to be so refined, she can be downright tacky at times."

"Yes, but Morgan put her in her place, but then he should not have. When people see us together they shouldn't see us as a mismatched couple. When a couple walks into the room and heads turn it should be for all the right reasons and not the wrong ones."

"And you see that happening?"

"Possibly. I have no problem with who I am, but I can't honestly think that I'm someone he'd probably consider as his ideal woman."

"Then why do you think he asked you out all those times?"

"Who knows? Maybe out of boredom."

"I don't think you're being fair to Morgan or to yourself." Kylie then leaned forward in her seat and sighed. "Do something for me, Lena."

"What?"

"Stop selling yourself short. When you get home take a look in the mirror. You're a beautiful full-figured African American woman who could walk into any room and put the Cassandra Tisdales of this world to shame, mainly because not only do you have outside beauty, you have inside beauty as well. Don't think a man like Morgan wouldn't know that. And I think you need to think about something."

"What?"

"What if you are Morgan's ideal woman? And what if he's that one man who doesn't care that you're your mother's primary caretaker? Then what?"

A small smile touched the corners of Lena's lips. "Then I'll get the hell out of Dodge quick like and in a hurry."

Kylie lifted a brow. "What does that mean?"

"It means that I would run like hell because I wouldn't know the first thing about handling a man like Morgan...sexually, I mean. I bet his testosterone level is probably close to hitting the Richter scale. I get hot all over at the thought of sleeping with him."

Kylie grinned as her eyes glittered teasingly. "So the thought has crossed your mind?"

A frisson of desire inched its way through Lena's bloodstream at the same moment she knew a heated flush was probably showing in her cheeks. "Yes, more than a few times a week. How about every day?" she said honestly.

Kylie laughed. "Now you know what I was going through after meeting Chance."

Yes, Lena thought. She knew. But she also knew that she and Kylie were different people. Kylie had started out being defiant and determined, but in the end she had given in to Chance's charm. Lena didn't intend to give in to any man's charm again. What Derek and others before him had done had more than pricked her pride. It had made her see things quite clear. And the more she kept her dealings with Morgan on a business level, the better things would be.

Chapter 5

Lena tried to recall her immunity to any man's charm as she gazed at the two beautiful bouquets of fresh flowers Morgan had just handed her. One for her and the other for her mother.

Finding herself unnerved, she glanced up at him. "Thanks for the flowers, Morgan. Please come in."

She moved aside when he stepped inside. While she closed the door she noticed him glancing around, and when their gazes connected again he said, "You have a nice place."

"Thanks. Please let me take your jacket." The

weather had changed and there was a brisk coolness in the air. The warm weather from earlier in the week was gone. In fact the forecasters had predicted the possibility of snow sometime next week.

"Mom's in the kitchen," she said, placing his leather jacket on the rack. "I told her you had arrived, so she should be coming out in a little bit. Can I get you something to drink?"

"No, I'm fine."

Because his brother was married to her best friend, she and Morgan were invited to some of the same functions on occasion, so she had seen him in casual wear before. But there was something about seeing him now, standing tall and handsome in her living room wearing a pair of jeans, a blue pullover sweater and a pair of comfortable-looking sneakers that made her wonder, and not for the first time, why he didn't have a steady girlfriend.

He was definitely one fine specimen of a man, a healthy-looking one at that, which meant he probably had a normal sex drive like most men. And not that she thought he went for the celibacy thing, but since being officially introduced to him at that charity ball over a year ago, she couldn't recall his name linked to any female. Now, with his brother Donovan it was a different story. The fun-loving Donovan Steele had a reputation around town as being a ladies' man.

"If you will excuse me I'm going to find a couple of vases for the flowers. Please make yourself at home."

"All right."

Although she was conscious of the tingly sensations that lit every cell in her body, Lena tried to ignore them as she quickly left the room. When she stepped into the kitchen she saw her mother, bending over the oven with an apron on. Lena had awakened that morning to the smell of fresh peaches cooking and had lain in bed for a while to make sure she was at the right house. Her mother hadn't set foot in the kitchen since they moved in almost five years ago, other than to eat. But her invitation to Morgan had nearly done the impossible.

"Did you get Morgan settled comfortably, dear?" her mother asked as if she had a pair of eyes in the back of her head.

"Yes, and he brought these for us."

Odessa straightened and turned around. Upon seeing the flowers she smiled. "Now, wasn't that real sweet of him?"

Lena shrugged, knowing that it was but not

wanting to give her mother any ideas where Morgan was concerned. "All the Steeles are nice, Mom."

"Yes, and Kylie's blessed to have met Chance. And just to think that Tiffany and Chance's son Marcus got them together."

Lena couldn't help but smile at how the two teenagers had successfully played matchmakers. She glanced over at the stove. "It seems you're serving more than just chicken and dumplings and peach cobbler," she said upon seeing all the pots.

"I decided since that young man hasn't had a good home-cooked meal in a while I would throw in a few more items. I really like him."

To Lena that fact was obvious and she couldn't help wondering why. Her mother had met Derek, Jon and Paul. They'd held conversations with her when they came to pick Lena up for dates, but neither of the three had won her mother over like Morgan to the point to bring her back into the kitchen.

"I'll be back in a second."

Lena watched as her mother left the kitchen to go to the living room and speak to Morgan. A few moments later she could actually hear Morgan's deep voice and her mother laughing about something. She wondered what that was all about, knowing before she left the sanctuary of the kitchen to find out she needed to pull herself together. It seemed Morgan Steele had a way with women, both young and old.

Her mother laughed out again, and then the laughter was followed by the sound of Morgan's voice. Lena paused as she put the flowers in the vase, as her mind, her thoughts and every sensation in her body focused on that voice. It was strong, husky, yet in some ways gentle. But then on the other hand, there was a sensuous quality about it that touched something deep inside her, in the most provocative places. There wasn't a nook, corner or crevice of her body that hadn't at one time or another been affected.

"Lena?"

She snapped out of her thoughts when she heard her mother call out her name. "Yes?" she called back.

"Morgan needs help setting the table."

Lena lifted her brow. Morgan was setting the table? She picked up the vases and walked out of the kitchen. She placed one vase in the middle of the dining room table and the other on a table in the living room. She glanced up and saw the white linen tablecloth in Morgan's hands.

"I guess Ms. Odessa is going to make me work for my supper," he said, smiling.

"At least I'm letting Lena help you," her mother replied, amused as she left them alone to go back into the kitchen.

"I like your mom, Lena. She's fun to be around."

Lena nodded, thinking it strange that none of the guys she'd brought home to meet her mother had ever made such an observation. "I don't know why Mom felt I needed to help you with this," she said, leading him into the dining room and removing the flowers off the table that she had put there mere minutes ago. "And you should feel honored you get dining room space. Usually our guests just cram with us in the kitchen."

"I wouldn't mind."

Lena glanced up at him, saw the sincerity in his eyes and knew that he would not have minded. That was one thing she had discovered about Morgan. He was so unlike Derek in that he didn't have a conceited bone in his body.

It didn't take them long to spread the linen covering over the table and smooth the center and sides. They worked quietly, not saying anything, and then suddenly they came up short upon realizing they had moved into the same area when they accidentally bumped into each other. His hands reached out, gripped her around the waist to steady her, and her body automatically went into an immobile mode; she felt suspended in space. The hands at her waist felt warm, strong yet gentle.

Breathing deeply, she tilted her head up and looked into his face, met his gaze and nearly got scorched from the deep, hot intensity from his eyes. That look alone overwhelmed her, made her pulse race and her breathing come out forced.

"Sorry," she muttered, quickly taking a step back. "I wasn't watching where I was going."

"No harm done. Neither was I," was Morgan's easy response…which was a lie, he thought. He'd been drawn to her scent like a bee drawn to honey.

"Dinner's ready. I need more hands to bring everything out," Odessa called out from the kitchen.

Thinking it would be best not to bump into her twice since he wouldn't be able to handle it, Morgan used his hand and gestured for her to go ahead of him and he followed her into the kitchen.

Morgan pushed away from the table with a huge smile on his face after finishing off a plate of Odessa's peach cobbler. He licked his lips. "That was the best peach cobbler I've ever eaten," he said. "My mom makes a banana pudding that's to die for, and I can see someone killing for your cobber as well, not to mention everything else you served today. Dinner was wonderful."

Over the rim of her iced tea glass, Lena watched the smile of pleasure that appeared on her mother's face, and shook her head. Morgan was a real charmer all right.

"I've eaten so much I'm going to have to trek around my neighborhood and walk it off," he added.

"No need to wait until you get home since Lena walks every day after dinner anyway. I'm sure she wouldn't mind the company."

Lena quickly gazed over at her mother, studying the older woman's innocent features. She couldn't help but wonder if her mother had hatched some crazy idea about her and Morgan getting together. First dinner and now a walk—just the two of them. "I'm sure Morgan has had enough of our company for one day, Mom, and wants to call it a day."

Morgan glanced over at her. "Quite the contrary. I enjoyed both of your company and I'd love going for a walk."

Think! Think! Lena tried unscrambling her mind to come up with a reason she couldn't go walking with him. All through dinner her naughty twin had tried to surface by putting all kinds of thoughts into her head. "It's kind of windy out. It will mess up my hair," she said, saying the first thing that popped into her head, although it sounded rather lame.

"Of course it's windy, Lena. It's March," her mother said, waving off her excuse with her hand.

"And there's a cap in my jacket you can borrow," Morgan tacked on.

Lena sighed. Both her mother and Morgan were looking at her expectantly, as if waiting for her to come up with another excuse. She smiled over at her mother but inwardly narrowed her eyes at Morgan. Why was he going along with Odessa on this? Just wait until they got outside. There was a lot she had to say to him.

"Fine," she said, standing. "Let me change into something more appropriate for walking."

Ten minutes later she returned to find Morgan had helped her mother clear the table. She found them in the kitchen, again sharing another joke. "I'm ready." At the sound of her voice they both turned and smiled, and from the sparkle in her mother's eyes Lena could tell she was in high spirits.

"Here's the cap I was telling you about," Morgan said, moving away from her mother to come stand in front of her. Instinctively, she reached out to take it from him, but instead of handing it to her he placed it on her head. He stepped back and then tipped his head to the side as if to admire his handiwork. "It will work. Looks good on you."

Lena decided she needed to see for herself. She walked a couple of steps out of the kitchen to look into the huge mirror that hung on the dining room wall. He was right. It work would and it looked good…if blue, black and silver were your colors and you supported the Carolina Panthers.

She turned around and saw that Morgan had followed her out of the kitchen and was leaning against the door fame. His muscular shoulders came close to filling the doorway. "You do know I'm not a Carolina native and that I was born and raised in New York. Buffalo in fact," she said, meeting his gaze, and a warm oozy feeling flowed through her bloodstream. That seemed to happen each and every time she looked into his eyes.

He smiled. "Is that a cute way of telling me that you prefer rooting for the Buffalo Bills?"

"Not necessarily. Lucky for you I quickly converted when the Panthers came to town."

"We native Carolinians do appreciate that," he said in a voice that was warm and engaging.

He straightened his stance. "Are you ready for our walk?"

"Yes." *Ready but not looking forward to it,* she thought further.

Instead of jogging or fast walking, they eased into a nice leisurely walk. Neither said anything for a long while, but Morgan was prepared for Lena to have a lot to say. He knew she hadn't liked the way her mother, with his help, had orchestrated this stroll.

Although it was windy, the sun was peeking through the clouds, making it a beautiful day the week before the first day of spring. Not that it mattered in Charlotte. Spring came when spring came. Last year it snowed on the first day of spring. Occasionally, they were visited by the snowstorm the locals called the Beast from the East. Last one had hit a couple of years ago, snowing everyone in the mountains, and surrounding areas, in for a few days.

Deciding they had walked long enough without conversation he decided to start one. "Nice day, isn't it?"

He watched Lena snatch her head around as if she'd forgotten he was there. It was his opinion that she looked downright cute, dressed in a green jogging suit and well-worn sneakers and wearing his cap. "Yes." She then resumed looking straight ahead, up the road, with her mouth shut.

His lips crinkled at the corners. If she thought he was going to let her get away with one-word responses, she had another thought coming. "Tell me in twenty-five words, but not less than ten, just what do you think is nice about it?"

She turned her head slightly, and he knew it was taking a lot of her willpower to keep her features expressionless. He could just imagine what she was thinking. When she didn't say anything he decided to coax her on. "Come on, Lena, you can do it. You're a Realtor so you have to be full of nice, descriptive words. Try it. I double-dare you."

Lena couldn't help the smile that spread across her features. For some strange reason she found Morgan's antics endearing. "Okay, let me tell you what's so nice about it…from a Realtor's viewpoint."

Smiling, he tilted his head downward to hers. "I'm listening."

"Well, there's the scent of spring in the air," she said, dimpling, then breathing in deeply. "That's always nice. Not to mention the brisk breeze that's not too cold. One of the reasons I bought a home in this area was for that lake over there," she said, pointing to the huge body of water that ran through the subdivision.

"I love walking around it, smelling all the dogwoods and seeing them bloom. But then, I need to be honest about something. Spring is nice but I like winter better mainly because I love snow."

He arched a brow, and a smile touched the corners of his lips. "You like snow?"

She returned his smile. "Yes. I love watching the snowflakes fall to the ground and cover everything. I like drinking a mug full of hot chocolate while standing at the window looking at the snow fall and wishing I could just go out there and play in it. At least that wasn't one of the things I had to give up moving from New York. Although I got to see snow more often while living in Buffalo, at least I still get to see it."

She glanced up in the sky and blinked against the sun's brightness and then back at him. "So, how did I do?"

"You went over your word count."

She stopped, tipped her head back and laughed; really laughed. Moments later she stuck her hands in her pockets and continued walking, shaking her head. "I would hate working for you."

He chuckled. "You already do."

Her head shot up and she stared at him with all amusement gone, wondering if he was trying to remind her of their relationship. "Sorry, I forgot."

This time it was Morgan who stopped walking. When she stopped as well, he reached out and lifted her chin with the tip of his finger. "I didn't say that to make you remember."

She shrugged. "That's okay."

Morgan felt the spell that had surrounded them for the past few moments trying to break, but a part of him refused to let it. She had started to relax around him and her mood had been light, almost carefree. He liked that.

"So what made you decide to leave New York to move to North Carolina?" he asked, wanting to get her talking again, as they resumed their walk. And he relaxed.

She didn't say anything for a while, and for a moment he wondered if she was going to answer. Then she said, "My dad. In my senior year of high school his health began failing and the doctors thought a change in climate would help him. So we moved here right after my graduation and I began attending the University of North Carolina. Dad died a month after my graduation from college."

"I'm sorry."

A small smile touched her lips. "So was I. He was a wonderful man and I loved him deeply."

She got quiet for a brief moment and then she continued by saying, "It was really hard for Mama. They had been together so long. There were too many memories in the house where we lived, so we eventually put it up for sale and bought this one. That helped some, but for a while I thought I was going to lose another parent when Mom went into a state of depression from all her grief."

He nodded. "How long did it last?"

She titled her head to look up at him. "Who says it has stopped? She has good days and bad days, and trust me when I say today was one of her good days, and I have to thank you for it. This is the happiest I've seen her in a long time. She actually cooked all of the dinner herself. I can't tell you the last time she went into a kitchen other than to eat or to get a drink of water."

"I can't accept your thanks because I don't know what I did. Your mother is a nice person and like I told you earlier, I like her. I can't imagine her getting depressed."

"Well, she does. And then there's her obsession with grandchildren. Did she mention anything about that to you?"

He smiled. "It just so happened that she did, briefly today while you were changing clothes and we were clearing the table. But that's okay. Like I said the other day, I think all mothers believe it's their duty to prod their children into parenthood."

Lena stopped walking. "So you think it's a phase that will pass?"

"Maybe. Maybe not. If not, then you might have to do some serious thinking as to what you want as well. And if you want a baby, too, then you're going to have to find a man who'd be more than willing to get you pregnant."

His voice was so low it could almost be defined as a whisper, and his words had sounded too serious. And the eyes staring down at her were more intense than ever.

Lena took a deep breath, inwardly forcing her naughty twin to behave when she felt her fingers itching to reach out and wrap her arms around his neck, bring his mouth down to hers and kiss him in all the ways she'd always dreamed about.

"Maybe we should head back now, Lena."

Morgan's words gave her the strength she

needed to regain full control. But for one fleeting moment she felt something had changed, shifted, gotten altered. As they began walking back toward her house she tried not to put too much emphasis on her surprise when he took her hand in his, making her aware of his touch, making her feel a little squeeze in her chest.

Today she would take this, the casual versus professional rapport they were sharing. When they saw each other again it would be business as usual. But today was nice and she planned on making today's pleasantries, as well as Morgan's own special blend of kindness, a very special memory.

Chapter 6

"We'll be able to finish up things once Morgan brings his attention back to the meeting."

Morgan snapped his head up to look into his older brother's intense dark eyes. He glanced around the room and saw that Bas, Donovan and Vanessa were staring at him as well. So okay. He'd been caught daydreaming. No big deal. But with the smirk he saw on Donovan's face he knew that his younger brother would make it a big deal. And Morgan didn't have long to wait.

"In defense of Morgan, he can't help that he

has a lot on his mind. The woman of his dreams, his *perfect* woman, still can't seem to notice that he's alive."

"Go to hell, Donovan," Morgan said, glaring over at his youngest brother.

"Okay, you two, knock it off. If you want to go at each other, save it for the next Saturday we're on the court," Chance said.

Morgan nodded. It was a family tradition that he and his three brothers got together every Saturday to play basketball, mainly to get rid of any competitive frustrations they might get from working together. Depending on the depth of their frustrations, the game could get downright mean and ugly. "My pleasure," he said, giving Donovan a look that clearly said...*next time we're on the court, your ass is grass.*

"Who's his perfect woman?" Of course Vanessa had to ask. At twenty-six she was the oldest of the three girl cousins and headed the PR department. It had been challenging for the Steele Brothers to keep an eye out for their younger female cousins while growing up, especially when Vanessa and her best friend from high school, Sienna Davis Bradford, were always getting into trouble.

"Lena Spears is his perfect woman," Donovan was more than happy to say.

A smile touched Vanessa's lips. "Lena Spears? I know her and she's a jewel. We've worked together on several community projects. Now, why doesn't she notice that Morgan is alive?"

"Can we get back to the meeting?" Morgan asked, deciding he didn't want his personal business discussed, especially if everyone had to hear Donovan's take on things.

"You mean you want to get back to the meeting that wasn't holding your attention anyway?" Bas said, rolling his eyes.

When Vanessa laughed, Morgan glared over at her. "Did I happen to mention that I was in Atlanta with Cameron a couple of weekends ago and he asked about you, Van?"

Morgan watched the amusement die on his cousin's face, knowing he'd said something that would shut her up for a while. All it took was the mere mention of Cameron Cody's name. Vanessa couldn't stand the man.

"Okay, knock it off, all of you," Chance said, taking the role as leader. "Let's get back down to business. We have important things to discuss."

An hour later when the meeting ended Morgan

was the first to stand and head for the door. "Where's the fire?" Bas called after him.

Morgan smiled as he kept walking. Oddly enough, he felt there was a fire. Every time he thought about Lena a part of him would erupt into a smoldering blaze. It didn't take much effort to recall their walk on Sunday. Even though there had been other people around walking and jogging, there had been something pleasingly intimate about strolling beside Lena, talking to her, listening to her talk. And on those occasions when their arms would occasionally brush, he'd felt a sharp sensation all the way to his toes.

He checked his watch as he stepped onto the elevator. His smile widened. Lena would be receiving a package from him in about an hour and he hoped that she liked her gift.

...If you want a baby, too, then you're going to have to find a man who'd be more than willing to get you pregnant....

Morgan's words from yesterday still weighed heavily in Lena's thoughts as she walked into her office. She would even admit that at one time she'd had thoughts of visiting a sperm bank. From a recent article she'd read in a magazine, more and more single professional women who were feeling the ticking of their biological clock were considering just that option. But of course being the ultra-traditional person she was, she had dissed the idea. She'd grown up in a home with both a loving father and mother and couldn't see cheating a child out of a chance to have that as well. That reasoning always put her back at square one.

"Good afternoon, Lena."

She smiled over at her secretary as she grabbed the mail off the table and began flipping through it. "And a good afternoon to you, Wendy. Did I get any calls?"

The woman, who was only a few years older, smiled back and said, "Not since the last time you checked earlier, but you did get a package. I put it on your desk."

"Thanks, it's probably those brochures I ordered last week," Lena said, tossing the junk mail in a basket to get shredded while keeping hold of anything she considered important. "I'll be in the back if you need me."

Entering her office, Lena removed her jacket and then took the time to hang it in the closet before taking a seat behind her desk. She eyed the box sitting in the middle of it, immediately thinking it definitely wasn't the brochures she had ordered. It was a beautiful gift box, wrapped in red satin-looking paper with a huge white bow.

She immediately pushed the button for Wendy.

"Yes, Lena?"

"Where did this box come from?"

"It was delivered to you today by a private courier."

Lena lifted a brow as she studied the box. There wasn't a card on the outside. "There's not a card."

"It's probably inside the box. You know, one of those ploys to keep nosy secretaries from reading it. Not that I would do such a thing," Wendy said, chuckling.

"So, you have no idea who sent it?" Lena asked.

"Don't you?" was Wendy's quick response. "It's your box."

Lena shook her head. "I don't have a clue, but there's only one way to find out."

"Wait! You want me to call for the bomb squad?"

"Real cute, Wendy." Lena chuckled as she hung up the phone thinking that her secretary was forever the comic, and Wendy's comment made Lena see just how paranoid she was being about the box.

Deciding she had wasted enough time as it was, she reached out and began opening it, not surprised when Wendy came into the room. "If there's an explosion we blow up together," her faithful secretary said. "But trust me, it's probably safe. The guy who delivered it was too cute to be on the wrong side of the law."

It was on Lena's tongue to say "whatever," but when she removed the tissue paper her heart caught as she pulled out a beautiful handcrafted snow globe. Inside was a miniature replica of Charlotte's skyline, and with a push of a small button, that skyline became covered as snowflakes seemed to drift from the sky over the city. Amazing.

A part of Lena's heart suddenly felt tight in her chest. She knew who had sent the package. Morgan. He had remembered her comments about the snow.

"Umm, it doesn't look like one of those explosive devices, so I guess we're safe," Wendy said, reclaiming her attention but only briefly.

"No, it doesn't and yes, we're safe." A few moments later she said, "Isn't it beautiful?" still in awe of her gift.

"Yes, if you like snow, and we all know that you're one of the few strange ones who do."

Lena chuckled as she looked back at the box and saw there was something else inside. She placed the snow globe on her desk and pulled out another item wrapped in tissue paper. When she had it uncovered she couldn't help but laugh. It was her very own Carolina Panthers cap. She then pulled out the card and it said:

Lena,
I saw the snow globe in a store today and it made me think of you. Hope you like it. And about the cap. I thought you looked so cute in mine that I wanted to get you one of your own. And I truly did enjoy our walk together on Sunday. We must do it again sometime.
Morgan

Emotions Lena wasn't ready for touched her at that moment. She couldn't recall the last time someone saw something in a store—other than an outfit Kylie might see that she would tell her about saying it would look good on her. But this was different. This was special. And it had come from a man. Definitely no man had ever taken the time to send her a gift such as this, one that reflected something she truly liked.

"Before I get back to work, is there something you want to share with me?"

Lena glanced up. She had forgotten Wendy

was still in the room. She pulled herself together and cleared her throat and said, "It's from Morgan Steele."

Her secretary and friend raised a curious brow. "And?"

"And I think it's time you got back to work."

A cute little frown, one that wasn't at all convincing, appeared on Wendy's face. "See if I share my next romance novel with you. From now on you're going to have to buy your own." With her head held high, Wendy then turned and walked out of the office, closing the door behind her.

Lena grinned as she turned her attention back to the snow globe and cap. She then read the note again. She didn't want to acknowledge the warmth she felt. She clenched her hands together trying to think logically and to fight both the tension and the excitement warring within her. A part of her, the woman in her, wanted to feel giddy at the thought that the very handsome Morgan Steele enjoyed the time he had spent with her walking on Sunday and wanted to do so again.

A part of her was too afraid to come out of her protective shell to believe such a thing. It had been that same part of her that had encouraged her to turn down his invitation to go out with him those other times. The way she saw it she had two strikes against her when it came to a man like Morgan. She wasn't the type of woman someone would associate him with dating, and although it appeared he and her mother got along great on Sunday, and he had even gone so far as to say he liked Odessa, she had no reason to believe he would be willing to take on a twosome if things were to get serious between them.

But then, there was her Gemini twin who was right there in her mind taunting with the questions...*But who wants serious? Even if there could never be a forever between you and Morgan, there could be a now. Why not just live each day at a time and take whatever you want?*

Lena knew the answers. She couldn't think that way because she was the sensible one. The one who thought things through before she acted.

Which was what she was driven to do now.

She needed to call and thank Morgan for the gifts. How should she approach that? Should she tell him how much receiving the gifts truly meant to her, or should she hide her true feelings and thank him, making no big deal of it, and move on?

She reached for the phone deciding to let her conscience be her guide. She took a deep breath to pull back in control, making sure it would be her conscience and not that of her naughty twin.

"Mr. Steele, Lena Spears is on the line for you."

Morgan smiled as he tossed the papers he'd been reading aside. "Please put her through, Linda, and hold the rest of my calls."

As soon as his secretary clicked Lena on the line, in a businesslike tone he said, "Morgan Steele."

"Morgan, this is Lena."

The moment he heard her voice, potent desire slid through every part of his body despite his best efforts to stop it from doing so. He inhaled softly and leaned back in his leather chair. "Lena, how are you?"

"I'm fine. I was calling to thank you for my gifts."

"You didn't have to do that."

"Yes, I did. It was very thoughtful of you."

He chuckled softly. "On occasion I try to be a thoughtful person."

"Well, you are. And there's also another reason I called. The developers of the Palisades and I are close to reaching an agreement about those additional amenities I'm pushing for. I've come up with a list and was wondering if you had the time for us to go over them."

He raised a brow. "Now?"

"Yes, now, unless you're busy at the moment."

Morgan looked at his closed briefcase, and then across the room at the golf club resting against the wall where he'd been practicing his swing. He definitely wasn't busy. Besides, it was time he made her an offer she couldn't refuse. Using his skill in the area of research and development, for the past couple of weeks he had been researching just what Lena wanted in her life, and without her knowing it he'd put a plan in place not just to develop those wants but to bring them into the limelight.

For now he needed to continue to stick with his plan, although he was about to sharpen his strategy. "Unfortunately, I'm rather busy at the moment. How about if we got together tomorrow?"

"Okay, when would be a good time for me to drop by your office?"

His office was the last place he intended for them to meet, especially when he presented his proposal to her. "My secretary mentioned earlier that my calendar for tomorrow is full and I'm flying out of town on business Wednesday morning and won't be returning until late Sunday. What about sometime later tomorrow, after my last appointment?"

"How late are we talking about?"

He knew she was asking because she had to pick up her mother from the adult day care center by six. "Let's say around four. You should be able to cover everything in a short while, right?"

"Yes."

"Good. And, Lena?"

"Yes?"

"My last appointment is out of the office on the other side of town. I prefer not driving back into this area if you don't mind. Is there another place where we can meet? What about your office?"

He knew from something she'd said last week that her office officially closed at four, which meant her secretary would have left for the day. Originally, he'd thought of some pretense to get her to his home and speak with her there, but the more he'd thought about, he'd concluded that although he wanted to be completely alone with her, he was willing to do so while on her turf if it would make her feel more comfortable and in control of the situation.

"My office?"

"Yes. Will that be a problem?"

She paused briefly, then said, "No. My office is fine. I'll look for you at four."

"All right. I'll see you then."

When Morgan hung up the phone he smiled broadly. Tomorrow couldn't get there fast enough to suit him.

Chapter 7

The next day was the busiest Lena had had in a long time. She was excited over a new sale, but on the other hand, every time she glanced at her watch or clock, butterflies would take off in her stomach to the point where she was about ready to pull her hair out. Just the thought that within hours Morgan would be arriving, invading her space, had her unsettled.

She had tried talking Wendy into working late, but since it was Wednesday, prayer meeting night at church, her friend had refused to stay, saying she needed all the prayers she could get to be blessed with a good man.

As Lena settled back in her chair to go over a new contact she'd acquired, her thoughts drifted to last night. Unlike with the other nights, it hadn't been her mother calling out for her dad that had awakened her. It had been an ache deep within her, gnawing away at her to the point it made her stomach tremble. She had wanted to blame it on nervous energy, but she knew it was more. The inner turmoil and fierce turbulence she'd felt had been a stark reminder of just how empty, unfulfilling and unsatisfying parts of her life were.

She was thirty-one, a relatively healthy young woman, single—a point her mother still reminded her of on occasion. She knew it downright bothered her mother that she didn't have a man in her life.

Maybe her naughty twin was right about some things. If she accepted that her life would remain as it was, then why couldn't she become involved in someone just for sanity's sake? It would be someone who on occasion would take her to dinner or a movie, someone who could be her escort to the different social functions she attended during the year, and someone who would eventually become her exclusive lover.

She tried recalling the last time she'd shared a bed with a man. Had it been over six years ago? Not since the death of her father? Sheesh! No wonder she was having sleepless nights with feelings of emptiness that wouldn't go away. She possessed a healthy sex drive like the next woman, and should she deny herself a relationship with a man just because she never intended to get serious about one?

She sighed deeply and rubbed the back of her neck, wondering if those were the thoughts of her naughty twin or thoughts of her own. For the first time in a long while she was convinced that she and her twin were on the same page. And she knew the reason.

Morgan Steele.

Morgan had a way of making her acutely aware that she was a woman, a living, breathing woman with real needs. Being around him at times unsettled her. All it took was one of his warm smiles, the sound of his deep husky voice or even one of those impersonal glances he could send her way to drum up heat deep inside her. He could look at you with an intensity that took your breath away, strip you of every wall you wanted to erect and pull you to him like metal to a magnet.

And those were the very reasons the thought of being alone with him today was so unnerving.

"I'm out of here, Lena."

Lena glanced up at the doorway and saw her secretary standing there smiling. She then glanced at the clock on her wall. "It's not four o'clock yet."

Wendy chuckled. "I know but I didn't take a lunch and decided to check out early to run by the cleaner's. Do you need anything before I leave?"

Yes, for you to knock some sense into me. Instead she said, "No, I'm fine here. I don't expect Morgan to stay long, so I should be leaving within a few minutes myself."

Wendy nodded. "Okay, then, I'll see you tomorrow."

Lena settled back in her chair and began making a list. She had placed Morgan's file on her desk. First they needed to discuss the amenities for the home he was interested in buying, and then they would go over the potential sale of his home. He would need to make a decision and soon as to whether or not he wanted to sell his house to the Edwardses or his brother Donovan. Then there was the decision of whether he wanted to place a binder on the new house contingent on selling his present one.

When she heard someone in the doorway, assuming it was Wendy, she didn't glance up when she asked, "Forget something?"

"No, I don't think I've forgotten anything."

Lena snatched her head up at the sound of the deep, masculine voice. She sucked in a deep breath at what now filled her vision. There standing in her doorway was Morgan with a sensuous air surrounding him. And he was staring at her with a very opulent look in his eyes. Today he appeared more overpowering than ever, and she met his stare with a leveled gaze while heat rushed through her body.

She released a shaky sigh and slowly stood to her feet. This was supposed to be a business meeting, but at that moment discussing business was the furthest thing from her mind.

He wanted her.

That thought was most prevalent in Morgan's mind as he tried to rein in his control, desires and temptation. Just looking at her did all sorts of things to him. But the last thing he wanted to do was give the impression that the only thing he was interested in was something physical.

He watched her come around her desk as if she

were floating on air, moving with sophistication, style and grace. Men who thought there wasn't anything sexy about a full-figured woman needed to take a second look. Here was a woman who was smart, confident and savvy. Combine all those things with a voluptuous figure and what you got was all the woman any man could possibly want.

He took a deep breath thinking that his first rule of seduction was to take control of the situation with authority, from beginning to end. In the past he'd made the mistake of letting Lena decide their future, but not anymore. By the time he left her office today he would have placed his stamp on at least one part of her.

Deciding to take things slow at first, he approached her with an outstretched hand. "Once again I appreciate your flexibility, Lena." From the relieved expression on her face he could tell that his businesslike air relaxed her.

"Morgan, I was glad to accommodate you."

One side of his mouth tilted into a deep smile. By the time it was over he would give new meaning to the word *accommodate*. "Shall we get down to business? I'm sure you have other things to do. And how's your mother?"

"She's doing fine."

"That's good. Do you mind if I remove my jacket?"

"No, not at all."

He took off his jacket and hung it on a rack before crossing the room and settling into the chair directly across from Lena's desk. He glanced around, liked the way her office was decorated and liked it even more that she had found a home for the snow globe. It was sitting on top of a bookcase, in eye view.

He also liked the comfortable-looking leather sofa in her office. "Nice sofa."

"Thanks."

"You ever use it?"

She raised a brow. "Use it for what?"

He shrugged. "For anything. The one in my office is mainly there for decoration, but Bas uses the one in his. In fact before he married he used to sleep on it a lot when he would work so late that he couldn't make it home. Of course all that changed after he got married."

She couldn't help but smile. "I would hope so. And to answer your question, my sofa is used a lot like yours, for decoration. I rarely stay late at the office to use it for anything else."

"I see."

When she took the chair behind her desk he didn't waste time asking, "So now, what about those amenities?"

For the next few minutes he listened as she talked, and he watched the movement of her mouth while she did so. She had such luscious lips and the thought of kissing them made his stomach quiver. The woman was temptation standing up, sitting down and he didn't want to imagine how much temptation she would be lying down.

"So there you have it, Morgan. The developers have agreed to everything I asked for but that one thing. They have also agreed to let the contract be contingent on you selling your house within a reasonable period of time."

He nodded. "Sounds like you've been busy looking out for my welfare," he said, leaning slightly forward, pinning her with his gaze.

Lena shivered, feeling the heat of that gaze. As usual he was dressed in a business suit. When he had taken off his jacket her gaze had been drawn to his broad shoulders. No matter what he wore, there was something masculine and virile in every outfit, always relaying a degree of inner strength. "Yes," she finally responded. "And I think the contingency is a good thing."

"Sounds like it is."

"Are you interested?"

Morgan suddenly caught her gaze and held it, and when he did so she suddenly began experiencing a strange sensation in the pit of her stomach. "Yes, I am very much interested," he said, not taking his eyes off her.

It was something in the way he'd made that statement that made her feel that perhaps they weren't talking about the same thing. With all the poise she could muster, she then stood to her feet. "Well, that's all I had to cover with you, Morgan."

He nodded. "There is this business proposition that I'd like to discuss with you, if you have the time."

She smiled as she settled back comfortably in her chair. "You have another house you want me to sell?"

"No, but it is something very important to me, something I've been thinking about for quite some time but kept putting off because there wasn't anyone I'd met that I felt comfortable about approaching to discuss a partnership."

Lena leaned forward. "Not even Cameron Cody? I understand the two of you are good friends and have done business together on several projects."

Morgan cleared his throat, cracked a smile and

chuckled. "Trust me, Cameron wouldn't work for this. I need a woman."

He watched her eyes reflect a myriad of questions before she repeated the last part of what he'd said. "A woman?"

"Yes. In order to pull things off successfully, I need a very astute businesswoman, someone with an open mind, who could think outside the box, and who will appreciate a golden opportunity. And I believe that you are just that person."

The charming smile on Morgan's lips almost had Lena agreeing to anything, without knowing exactly what this "business venture" was about. His eyes were hooked on hers, and somehow she felt his keen sense of intelligence as well as his single-minded determination. He had piqued her curiosity and she definitely needed him to elaborate. "Just what type of business proposition are you talking about, Morgan?"

Morgan leaned forward a little, making sure he had her absolute attention. He also wanted to be right there, to gauge her reaction to his words. "I want you to marry me and have my baby."

Dead silence.

Morgan studied her expression as she sat perfectly still. He saw her blink, then witnessed the fine arching of her brow; and mere seconds later he became an ardent observer of how her lips trembled slightly at the corner. His gaze then moved back to her eyes and saw how they slowly narrowed to sharp slits. Her expression left no doubt in his mind what he'd just told her wasn't anything like what she'd expected.

"Excuse me. I must have heard you wrong," she finally said, not taking her eyes off his.

"No, you heard me right, Lena."

She stared, as if what he'd said didn't make sense and she was imagining things. Then she spoke as she straightened up in her chair. "In that case, I need you to explain why you think I'd be interested in involving myself in something so preposterous."

He smiled. "Is it really preposterous? Think about it for a second. It's no different than a couple agreeing to a prenupt. Marriages of convenience, or more simply put, the one I'm interested in, a marriage of purpose, are not unheard of these days. People are marrying for a lot of reasons. Not everyone who marries is doing so for love."

Lena heard what he was saying and a part of her was a little disappointed. She had been the product of a couple who loved each other dearly, and when she had met his parents at Kylie's wedding, she had thought the same thing about them. And if she'd ever married, it was to have been for love. But then, she had given up the idea of ever marrying, so her feelings or lack of feelings were really a moot point.

However, she couldn't understand why Morgan of all people would settle for a loveless marriage when his two older brothers had married for love. Chance and Sebastian were so head over heels in love with their wives that it wasn't funny. Was there a reason Morgan intended to fight the same fate?

"All of that may be true, Morgan, but why are you willing to settle for less than love? You're good-looking, a successful businessman and you have a good personality. I think any woman would find you marriage material."

He chuckled. "Thanks, but the question is, would I find them wife material? I have a lot going on in my life. The last thing I need is drama, or getting into a situation I'd be trying to get out of a few weeks after the wedding. And not to put your gender down because there are some in mine that are just as bad, possibly even worse, but there are some women who're conniving, vicious, manipulative and looking to marriage as a way to secure their financial future. I don't have a problem with the latter, but I want that individual to be one of my choosing and not the other way around."

"And you actually see me as that person?"

"Yes. You bring a lot to the table. You're mature in your thinking, you don't have time for games or drama, but more importantly, I think you will make any child a wonderful mother."

She tried not letting his words be the confidence booster that they were. "What makes you think that?"

He shrugged. "I just do. Maybe it's a hidden insight I have, but just from talking to you I know you want a child, and I believe you will do right by one."

Yes, she did want a child, and staring thirty-two in the face wasn't a joke. But still, there was a lot to consider.

"And," he said, interrupting her thoughts. "I think you would make me a good wife."

Now, that got her attention. "Really, Morgan, like I said, there are plenty of women who will—"

"I don't want any of them."

"And you want me to believe that you want me?"

"Yes."

Lena's heart began pounding. She shook her head. This was crazy. What Morgan was proposing was ludicrous.

He leaned forward with his forearms resting on her desk. "Before you turn me down flat, let me tell you what I'll be offering you. First there's financial security, which I know is something that's important to you. Then there's companionship. I like you and you can consider me as a live-in buddy and pal, which is a relationship some married couples don't even have. I have no reason not to think we wouldn't get along. Then there's the baby, which is something I want and so do you. Last but not least is your mother."

Lena's spine stiffened. "What about my mother?"

"I have no problem with her becoming a part of our household. In fact, I more than welcome it. I think Odessa is special and want her to be my child's grandmother as much as I want you as my child's mother."

Lena bit her lip. Of all the selling points he'd presented to her, this was the one that touched her the most and she couldn't help the warm flood of emotions that suddenly flowed through her. No other male in her past had even as much as wanted her mother as part of their lives, let alone wanted to include her in their family fold.

"Lena?"

She met his gaze. "Yes?"

"I know what I'm asking might sound a bit unorthodox, but it's the way I want to do things. I would want us to marry as soon as possible and start working on the baby right away."

Lena's heart lurched, as heat swirled around in her stomach. "Start on the baby right away?"

"Yes, after the wedding of course. And another thing, only the two of us can know our marriage is not the traditional one, which means I want us to share a bed."

The startled look on her face let him know that she hadn't thought about that part of the arrangement. He decided to press on. "Just so you'll know, I'm thinking about going with that last home you showed me because it will be perfect for our family—which includes your mother. It will give her the privacy she needs while at the same time assuring her that she is wanted. It's important to me that she feels that she is a part of our lives and not an outsider."

Lena sighed. Morgan was hitting her at all angles and using every single argument she would come up with to his advantage. He was right. Financial security was something she craved, and more than anything she did want a child of her own. And her mother being part of her marriage rather than an outcast was more important than anything. But still…

"What if things don't work out?" she asked softly.

Morgan smiled. Now was not the time to tell her that things *would* work out. Once he got her in his bed, made love to her the way he'd dreamt of doing for over a year and lavished her with all the attention and respect she deserved, then she wouldn't want to be anywhere else.

Instead he said, "We can draw up an agreement that we will stay together and make things work for at least twelve months. After that time if you or I feel that marrying was a mistake, we will end the marriage with joint custody of our child."

He watched as Lena inhaled deeply before she said, "I need to think about this."

"Of course. Do you think you can have an answer by the time I return on Sunday? That's five days away."

Lena's chest tightened. She had a lot of thinking to do, and five days wasn't a lot of time. But still, she would have an answer for him. "Yes, I should have a decision for you by then."

"Good." He stood. "I'm on my way to grab something to eat at the Racetrack Café. Would you care to join me?"

Lena shook her head. The last thing she needed was something to eat. What she needed was time alone to think. "No, but thanks for asking."

"You're welcome." He crossed the room to get his jacket, and she came from around her desk. She decided to ask him the question she'd been pondering since he had arrived. "How did you get in here?"

"Your secretary," he said, slipping into his jacket. "I was walking in when she was leaving."

"Oh."

He smiled. "Was she supposed to hang around and announce me or something?"

"No, I was just surprised when you arrived," she said, walking him to her office door.

He raised a dark brow quizzically. "Had you forgotten about our appointment?"

Hardly. "No, I hadn't forgotten."

Now she stood in front of him at the door, and as usual he appeared overwhelming and his eyes were on her, as if he was studying her for some reason. The intensity of his gaze made her flush. "You're going to St. Louis, right?" she nervously asked.

He nodded. "Yes. You still have that business card I gave you with my cell phone number and e-mail address in case something comes up or if you need to ask me anything about my proposal?"

"Yes, and you still have mine, right?"

"Yes, I still have it."

"Well, don't hesitate to contact me if you want to withdraw your offer of the marriage thing."

He chuckled. "I won't be withdrawing it."

Lena toyed with the button on her jacket thinking he sounded pretty sure of that. "I hope you have a safe flight, Morgan."

"Thanks, and I promise to have an answer for you regarding the sale of my house when I return."

"Okay. Although I've been showing the Edwardses other places, I think they like your house the best."

The smile that tilted his lips widened. "That's good to know. I'll keep that in mind when I make my decision, and I hope you keep it in mind when you make yours."

Lena sighed, trying to ignore the intense stare in Morgan's eyes. She held out her hand. "Goodbye, Morgan. I'll see you in a few days."

He didn't take her outstretched hand. Instead he continued to stare at her, hold her gaze, rattling her already shaken composure. "I want to do things different this time, Lena," he said, his voice low, seductive.

Mesmerized, she dropped her hand to her side.

Her palm suddenly felt warm and sweaty. And when he took a step closer to her, an aching need, that throbbing desire that had awakened her last night, was there, clawing at her, and she took a step forward as well.

"I think we can do better than that," he said in a warm, husky tone, which was barely above a whisper, pulling her total concentration back in.

Before she could release her next breath, he lowered his mouth to hers with a quick, clean sweep of his tongue across her lips. He captivated her then and there, snapping her composure and destroying the last hold she had on her control.

She placed her hand on his chest when his mouth closed hungrily, greedily over hers, almost eating her alive and unleashing a degree of passion she didn't know she had. Her naughty twin had passion, yes, but her, no. But this was not her twin who felt the smoldering eruption deep inside her as Morgan's tongue sent her senses reeling from the mastery of his lips.

Nor was it her twin whose moans escaped her lips beneath Morgan's demanding mouth while he grasped her around the waist in a tight hold of possession, bringing her closer to him and making her aware of how masculine and strong his body was.

A part of her was totally stunned at the depth of her need, her passion, her desire, but then another part wasn't. The recesses of her mind taunted that this was Morgan, the man who had invaded her dreams for the past year. Morgan, who practically made her catch her breath every time she saw him. Morgan, the man who wanted to give her the baby she'd always wanted; and Morgan, the man her body was instinctively, unashamedly arching against.

She uttered a low moan of protest when he finally raised his head, and when he pressed her face against his chest she realized the impact the kiss had had on him as well. She heard his heart racing, felt the irregular beats beneath her head and heard the sound of his ragged breathing being forced from his throat. She buried her face deeper into his chest, feeling warm and contented. Moments later she sighed when she felt him rest his chin on the crown on her head.

They stood that way for a while, neither ready to separate, too mesmerized and filled with raw emotions to say anything. Then he reached down and lifted her chin with the tip of his finger, meeting her gaze, and then lowered his mouth to hers again. This kiss was gentler but was filled with a high degree of passion nonetheless.

When he finally released her mouth again, he let out a shaky breath and murmured softly, "I'd better go and please think about my proposal."

Placing one quick kiss to her lips, he turned and then he was gone.

Chapter 8

"Morgan asked you what!" Kylie asked, staring at Lena disbelievingly.

Lena waited until the waitress had placed her order of French fries on the table and walked away before directing her attention back to Kylie. "I know it sounds crazy but he asked me to marry him and have his baby."

Kylie continued to stare at her, saying nothing, and then she shook her head, smiling as she plucked a fry off Lena's plate. "So you're it."

Lena lifted a confused brow. "I'm what?"

"Morgan's perfect woman."

Lena frowned. "I have no idea what you're talking about."

Kylie scooted in her chair closer to the table so her voice wouldn't carry. At least she scooted as close as her huge stomach would allow. "Everyone in the Steele family knows about Morgan's obsession with finding the perfect woman. Evidently, you've made quite an impression on him."

"Or he's realized there's no such thing as a perfect woman, like there's no perfect man. But that doesn't explain why he wants that person to be me."

Kylie rolled her eyes. "Aw, come on, Lena. Morgan has shown interest in you since that night the two of you met at that charity ball. He asked you out several times but you turned him down."

Lena munched on her fry thinking that yes, he had asked her out, but she really hadn't taken him seriously at first. But when he'd asked a few more times she thought it would be a smart move to break things down to him as to why she wouldn't go out with him. Now he was asking her not only to marry him but also to have his baby.

"So, are you going to do it?"

Kylie's question interrupted her thoughts. She knew of all people, she had to be totally honest with her best friend. "Would I sound like an awful person if I said I was really thinking about the idea? Gosh, Kylie, he's the first man to take Mom into consideration. He actually said he would be proud to have her for his child's grandmother."

"Wow, that's deep, isn't it?"

"Yes, for me it is." Another thing that was deep was the kiss they'd shared. Even now if she were to touch her lips with her fingertips, she was convinced she would still be able to feel the warmth of Morgan's lips there. "But there are other things to consider," she finally said, sighing.

"Like what?"

"Although our union will be a marriage of purpose, as he put it, he still wants us to project a semblance of realness. In other words, he has no qualms about us sharing a bed."

"But you do?"

"Yes. No. Hell, I don't know." The last couple of guys she'd dated—way back when—took that time to cross her mind. They hadn't done anything to light a fire within her, at least not to the degree Morgan had with just a mere kiss. "Trust me, it wouldn't bother me one bit to sleep with Morgan," she finally said. "But what if we start something that neither of us can finish?"

"Meaning?"

"What if things don't work out and he decides I'm not the woman he wants to live with or the right woman for the mother of his child?"

Kylie shrugged. "Knowing Morgan I'm sure he's thought this thing through before approaching you with it. If I were you, the only thing I'd worry about is what decision I'll be giving him in five days."

She hadn't dreamed today, Lena thought, slipping beneath the covers later that night. She lay on her back and stared up at the ceiling as memories flooded her. It was hard to believe Morgan had actually asked her to marry him and have his baby.

After Morgan had left her office she had hung back, unable to leave as she'd planned to do. Instead she had sat at her desk trying to rationalize what had happened moments earlier, replaying in her mind his every word, every stroke of his tongue in her mouth.

In the end when she'd realized she hadn't been hallucinating, she had called Kylie and asked to meet her at the nearest Burger King after she closed her florist shop that day.

After their talk she had left to pick up her mother from day care, barely remembering what their conversation had been about on the ride home. The only thing she remembered was the one single question that was still floating around in her head.

Why, of all the women he knew, he wanted to marry her?

From the day she had agreed to sell his house and help him locate another one, things had been strictly business between them. Even when he'd had dinner with her and her mother on Sunday he hadn't shown any obvious signs that he was attracted to her.

Or had he?

She had noted the intense looks in his gazes, but he'd always looked at her that way. In the past she had chalked things up as a one-sided attraction that she could never act on…but today, following his lead, she had.

She doubted that she would ever be able to look him in the face and not be reminded of their kiss. Today she had been introduced to another facet of Morgan's unique personality. His passionate side. It would be a side she would be constantly exposed to if they were to marry. Sheesh! For over a year he had been her nightly dream and she wasn't sure she was ready for him to make the jump from being her Mr. Fantasy to taking on the role of her Mr. Reality.

But then, all she had to do was close her eyes to remember the exact moment he'd made his outlandish proposal. *"I want you to marry me and have my baby."* The moment he had said the words, although she hadn't been sure she'd heard him correctly, he had looked at her with that deep, dark gaze of his as a spark of desire had flooded her insides, overheating her senses. And the seductive scent of the cologne he'd been wearing hadn't helped matters.

And later, right before he had left, he had taken the initiative to step closer to her, and she had boldly walked into his arms. And the exact moment their tongues had mingled, zapping her willpower with tenderness, she had known she was a goner. She knew even now that she would probably be whispering his name in her sleep. But that was okay. She didn't know of any other man whose name she'd rather whisper.

And as she closed her eyes to peaceful slumber, it was Morgan's face that occupied her dreams.

Morgan inhaled a steadying breath as he pushed himself out of bed and sat on the edge of it. The kiss he had shared earlier that day with Lena was still heavily on his mind, in his thoughts, embedded so deep in his memory that he couldn't sleep and was so elemental it made his entire body ache.

The kiss had been everything he had known it would be and more, and she had felt just like he'd figured she would in his arms. Now his senses were incapable of any other thoughts but those of her. At this point if she were to turn down his proposal to marry him and have his baby he didn't know what he would do.

He stood, deciding there wasn't much hope of getting a lot of sleep tonight. His only hope was to try and get some shut-eye on the plane, which he would be catching in a few hours. Throwing on his robe, he made his way down the stairs to get a cup of coffee before going over some paperwork for his meeting with Cameron and Ben Malloy.

Malloy was an entrepreneur with multifaceted interests. A year ago Morgan had approached him and Cameron in regards to what he saw not only as a sound business opportunity but also as a way to give back to his hometown's dying community. His latest venture was to open several shopping malls within urban areas of several handpicked communities around the country.

In recent years there had been an explosion of growth within the suburban areas of various cities, but there seemed to be a constant neglect within the downtown areas—where a number of African Americans lived. Most business owners—although they considered themselves rather astute—failed to recognize or acknowledge the potential growth in urban areas, and as a result, their narrow-mindedness had left the residents, those people living in the neglected areas, with limited access to shopping, adequate housing and entertainment.

Magic Johnson had brought attention to this issue when he opened several theaters within the urban communities across the country. And what Morgan, Cameron and Ben were posed to do was something similar with the development of a mall in St. Louis. Ben had asked their support and their aid in pouring a substantial amount of money into the project, and after doing a considerable amount of research they had determined it not only would be a worthwhile financial investment, but it would also be a way to help place development in those overlooked areas.

Morgan glanced at the clock when he entered his kitchen. It was three in the morning and he had a flight out at eight. After he'd left Lena he had come home to pack, prepare a quick dinner and savor the memories of his first kiss with the woman of his dreams.

Moments later as he sat at his desk, he absently stirred his coffee while trying to read the report Cameron's secretary had faxed earlier. Instead of concentrating, his mind was stuck on other things, namely Lena. Would she agree to his offer of marriage? He smiled thinking once he had her in his bed there were no limitations to just what he could do and would do.

The die was cast and an indescribable warmth spread through him in knowing that if Lena agreed to become his wife and the mother of his child, he would have her right where he wanted her.

Chapter 9

"How's that Steele boy?"

Lena smiled as she shoved in her briefcase the documents she needed to go over with a potential buyer. Funny, although she knew her mother's usage of the word *boy* was just a term, Lena couldn't visualize Morgan as a boy. She saw the person who had kissed her almost senseless yesterday as being a man in every full sense of the word.

"If you're asking about Morgan, I guess he's fine," she said, trying to keep her voice light, neutral and nonchalant.

"So when will he be coming back?"

Lena lifted her head and met her mother's gaze with an arched brow. "How did you know he was going somewhere?"

"He told me when he called a few days ago," Odessa said, as she sat at the kitchen table and took a sip of her coffee.

Lena, with an incredulous look on her face, shut her briefcase with a click. "Morgan called you?"

"Yes."

"When?"

"I told you it was a few days ago. Monday, I believe."

Lena sighed. "And *when* did he call on Monday?"

"In the afternoon. Before you got home."

Lena leaned against the kitchen counter. "He called to tell you he was leaving town?"

"No. Actually he called to thank me for dinner on Sunday, and then he mentioned he was leaving town." Her mother took another sip of her coffee, then asked, "Why all the questions?"

Lena rolled her eyes heavenward wondering if her mother had forgotten that she was the one who'd brought up Morgan in the first place. She decided to jog her memory. "Mom, you're the one who asked about Morgan. If you had spoken to him this week, then why did you even ask me how he was doing?"

"Because I thought that perhaps you had talked to him since then."

"Yes, I saw him yesterday at my office. You know I'm selling his home and helping him find another." Until she decided how she would handle his proposal she didn't want her mother to get any ideas, so she added, "Our relationship is strictly professional."

"If that's true, then why did he come to dinner?"

Lena sighed. "Because you asked him, and like he told you, he hadn't eaten a home-cooked meal in a long time. No man would have turned that down."

"Maybe, but I think he came for another reason altogether," Odessa said, matter-of-factly.

"And what reason is that?"

Her mother's lips parted into the barest of smiles. "You. That Steele boy likes you. Any fool can see that."

Later that day Lena's mind was filled with Morgan's proposition. He would see their marriage as a business venture. Could she do the same? What if she began developing feelings for him and he walked in one day and declared that he wanted out of the marriage? What would she do then?

She was jolted from her thoughts with the ringing of her telephone. She picked it up. "Yes, Wendy?"

"Vanessa Steele is on the line for you."

Lena raised a brow. She and Vanessa had worked together on several community projects around town. Like her own father, Vanessa's father had been the victim of cancer, so it wasn't unusual for them to participate in fund-raising activities to benefit the American Cancer Society. The same thing applied to Chance, whose first wife had died from cancer.

Lena liked Vanessa. She thought she was a person who wasn't just beautiful on the outside but on the inside as well. And unlike some people whose family had a lot of money—namely someone like Cassandra Tisdale—Vanessa Steele didn't have a "better than thou" bone in her body.

"Thanks, Wendy, please put her through."

Lena only had to wait a few moments before the sound of Vanessa's exuberant voice came on the line. "Lena, how are you?"

"I'm fine, Vanessa, and how are you?"

"I'm doing great. I just got a call from the principal at the high school I graduated from requesting that I spearhead this project, and after hearing it, I immediately thought of soliciting your,

Jocelyn's and Sienna's help." She chuckled, then added, "Kylie's pregnancy saved her from me pulling her in as well, and we don't have a lot of time to pull this thing together."

Lena's interest was piqued after hearing the excitement in Vanessa's voice. "What sort of project is it?"

"A mini career fair. Only thing is that the head of the school's business department wants it held in a few weeks. If we wait until next month we'll be competing against prom time. Sorry for the late notice but it was something she thought of doing just last night, but I think it's a wonderful idea to showcase local employment opportunities for those who might not be considering college as an option right now."

"I agree, it's a wonderful idea. How can I help?"

"I'm going to need your business to participate by having a booth. It would be nice for the students to see the wonderful opportunities in real estate."

"Do you have a date picked out yet?"

"Yes, the thirtieth of this month. That's a Friday. I've talked to Chance, and to kick things off the Steele Corporation will host a sit-down dinner for all the businesses that will be participating."

"Well, consider me in," Lena said, smiling.

"And consider it done. I'd like to have a meeting this weekend, something informal. How about my place on Saturday evening? Are you available?"

Lena didn't like to commit herself to being somewhere until she made sure her mother would be fine staying alone. So far her mother's condition had improved over the past month or so, and she was taking her medication when she was supposed to, making it easier for her to get around. "Let me get back with you about that meeting on Saturday."

"That's fine. Do you still have my number?"

Lena quickly checked the Rolodex on her desk. "Yes, I still have it."

"Good. I hope to see you if you can make it. If you can't I'll understand and I will call you the early part of next week and go over what was discussed."

"Thanks."

After hanging up the phone, Lena couldn't help but feel good that Vanessa had included her on the committee.

Morgan entered his hotel room after having dinner with Cameron and Ben. Moments later he had set up his laptop on the desk in the room and called home to speak with Chance before going into the bathroom to take a shower.

According to Chance, things were running smoothly back at the office, and Chance was glad to hear that Morgan would be returning home late Friday night instead of Sunday. That meant he would be home for the brothers' weekly basketball game Saturday morning.

After his shower, Morgan sat down at the desk and booted up his computer, immediately checking his e-mail to see if his secretary had sent him the documents he had requested of her earlier. She had, and after downloading all the attachments and reading through most of them, which took almost a full hour, he clicked on his Instant Messages, mainly to see if Donovan was online. His younger brother had a tendency to pick up dates online as well as off.

It appeared Donovan wasn't, but someone else was, he thought, when Lena's screen name popped up. He glanced at the clock radio near the bed. It was almost two in the morning. What was she still doing up?

He remembered her once mentioning that because of her mom, she typically got into bed early. He hoped that whatever reason she was still awake and on her laptop he wouldn't interrupt, because he intended to drop in.

* * *

Lena smiled as she continued to read the messages her goddaughter, Tiffany, had sent her earlier that day over the computer. Tiffany was excited about the prospect of becoming a big sister to a baby girl or boy, and before going to bed each night she would send Lena information on all the things she planned to do in her new role.

Tiffany had also written to tell her about this guy from school that she simply adored. Although Kylie had lightened up some on Tiffany now that she was sixteen, her best friend was still trying to make sure Tiffany didn't make the same mistakes she had made as a teen, which was understandable. These days Kylie was handling the situation in a different way, one that would not alienate her daughter. Chance and Kylie, along with Tiffany and Chase's son, Marcus, were one big happy family.

Lena leaned back against the headboard and balanced her laptop on raised knees, remembering what had awakened her at two in the morning. She had had a dream of her and Morgan together, in bed. A shiver ran down her spine at the memory.

In her dream Morgan's kisses had been just as heated as the one in her office. And when he had placed her on the bed, she had watched as his eyes changed from a dark brown to a hot brown as she succumbed to his magnetic pull and sexual appeal. Her breath had become shallow as he slowly removed her clothes, and desire consumed her, sending blood gushing through her veins like water through a fire hose. The eyes that had stared at her while he'd gotten undressed had had her pulse escalating, had made a certain part of her beg for him to take her over the edge. Her tension had mounted when he placed his body over hers, the scent of him sending her senses into overdrive. Her thighs had parted, and mere seconds before he was to enter her she had heard her mother cry out for her father, thus shattering the moment.

Lena sighed, thinking maybe that had been a good thing. She couldn't imagine how things would have been if Morgan had completed the task and made love to her. She was about to log off the computer when an Instant Message popped up on her screen, almost startling her. The message asked *What are you doing up so late?*

She frowned, lifting a brow, pondering the identity of the individual who wanted to know. She was not a person who indulged in Internet chats or instant messages unless it was Kylie or Tiffany, and she knew both of them were in bed asleep now. Her gaze was drawn to the screen name, and her heart almost stopped—*MDSteele*. She immediately sucked in a huge breath upon recognizing the screen name belonged to Morgan Darien Steele.

Ignoring the sensations that shivered up her spine, she nervously typed a response, wanting to make sure it was him.

Morgan?

Yes, it's me.

Satisfied, she then clicked further to answer his question. *Mom woke me. Bad dream. And I couldn't go back to sleep.* She decided not to tell him about his part in her sleepless night. *What about you? Why are you still up?*

Late business meeting and not ready to go to bed, was his typed response. And then *Is your Mom okay?*

Yes, she's fine. And how are things going with your meeting?

All right.

Moments later she typed. *Can I ask you something?*

You can ask me anything.

Why me, Morgan?

He knew what she was asking him and

moments later he typed *Why not you, Lena? You're a very beautiful and desirable woman and I want you.*

She swallowed hard, trying to keep her heart from pounding at his words. She refused to put too much stock into them. She was glad he couldn't hear her low laugh as she typed *Come on, Morgan, be for real. I'm not your type.*

And what do you see as my type?

Lena frowned. If he wanted the truth she would give it to him. *Worldly, highly sophisticated, pencil thin...*

Wrong on all accounts. Is that why you never wanted to go out with me?

She quickly typed a response. *No. I told you the reason. Once burned you learn not to play with fire.*

And you saw me as fire?

Maybe not fire, but definitely someone too hot to handle.

She could tell by the timing that he had paused before sending her his next typed response. *What if I told you that I saw you as someone too hot to handle as well?*

Lena smiled. *Then my response would be that you probably had me mixed up with my twin.*

You have a twin?

I'm a Gemini.

Interesting. What's the difference in the two of you?

I'm not a risk taker. My twin is. She lives for the moment without thinking about her actions. I do just the opposite. She decided to leave off anything about her twin having a tendency to be naughty and wild.

How often does she come out?

Lena rolled her eyes and grinned. Of course as a man Morgan would be interested in knowing that. *She's never actually come out. I've managed to keep her in line.*

What a shame.

Yes, well, that's how it is. And with that said, I'm going to turn in now. I'm finally feeling sleepy.

All right. Pleasant dreams. Good night, Lena.

Good night, Morgan.

Morgan smiled when Lena clicked off-line, and moments later he logged off his computer as well. He found it interesting what she'd told him about her so-called twin. Hmm, so there was another side of her, a side she was suppressing, a side where she could become another person, one who wouldn't hesitate to let her hair down.

He would love to meet that Lena Spears.

Now she had him curious and his pulse began racing. Just the thought of a loose Lena had him reaching for one of the chilled bottled waters the housekeeping staff had left in the ice bucket on the desk. He quickly opened it and took a sip, cooling his insides.

He shook his head, remembering when she'd mentioned she hadn't thought she was his type. He definitely had to prove her wrong on that, and while doing so he wanted to prove to her that whether she was the ultraconservative Lena or the not so conservative one, she was the woman he wanted.

Over breakfast the next morning Lena thought about her tête-à-tête with Morgan via her laptop. She hated to admit it but she'd actually enjoyed herself. There had been something downright fun about exchanging words with him online rather than by phone or in person. While online he couldn't hear her responses or see her facial expressions. She couldn't believe that she'd actually mentioned her mischievous twin to him. Well, he'd certainly seemed interested in that.

"I'm sorry I woke you last night, Lena."

Lena glanced up when her mother came to the table and sat down. Of all the times her mother had awakened her during the night, this was the first time she had apologized for doing so, and Lena wanted to assure her that there was no need for the apology. "Mom, you don't have to apologize, I understand."

Her mother looked at her with sad eyes. "And what do you understand?"

Lena shrugged. "I understand that you and Dad had a close relationship and that losing him was hard on you, and it still is. I know he was your very best friend and confidant. What the two of you shared was really awesome when you think about it."

Odessa nodded slowly and Lena saw the lone tear that clung to one of her eyelids. "I know you probably think at some point I should let go and move on with my life, Lena, but it's hard. Your father was my life. I feel lonesome without him. I know you're here but it's not the same."

Lena didn't know what to say. One of the main reasons she took her mother to the adult day care center twice a week was so she could be around other senior adults. Deciding to change the subject to a cheerier note, she asked, "So, how's Ms. Emily doing?" She watched a smile appear on her mother's lips.

"Emily is doing fine. I think this is the weekend her grandkids and great-grands are coming over."

Lena swallowed. Now she wished she hadn't brought Ms. Emily up. "Is it?"

"Yes. And I hope some nice young man comes into your life. I want you to share with a man that special love me and your father had. And then more than anything, I wish I could have a little one to cuddle on my knee before the good Lord calls me home."

An ache appeared in Lena's chest as she heard the sadness in her mother's voice. Considering everything, Lena knew that if she was to say yes to Morgan's proposal she would be able to give her mother the one thing she wanted the most.

Later that night after making sure her mother was settled in for the night, Lena took a shower and then slipped into a pair of silky pajamas Kylie had given her on her last birthday.

She settled in bed with her laptop, deciding to see if Tiffany had sent her a message that day. Today had been hectic, and to keep Morgan off her mind she had thrown herself into her work. She had shown another couple Morgan's house, and the moment she had walked through the door sensations had curled in the pit of her stomach, as if she expected to look up and see him walk down his stairs at any moment.

Unfortunately the couple she'd shown the house to had a three-year-old son who had just finished eating a chocolate bar. Needless to say, a chocolate handprint had gotten on a few of Morgan's doors. The boy's mother had apologized and wiped off those areas, but sometime tomorrow, Lena intended to go to Morgan's place and make sure the woman hadn't missed any spots.

Moments later she chuckled after reading Tiffany's note. The boy she had thought she was interested in a few days ago was no longer the hunk of the week. A new guy at school had caught her eye. Lena shook her head. Her goddaughter was a lot different from Kylie when she'd been that age. At sixteen, Kylie had thought Tiffany's father, Sam Miller, was her entire world. At least she'd thought that until he'd left her alone and pregnant. A part of Lena was glad that Tiffany was not getting serious about any one guy.

Lena tried not to notice that Morgan was also online. Chances were he was aware she was on the computer as well and she couldn't help wondering if he would do as he'd done the night before and engage in online conversation with her. She didn't have long to wonder when Morgan's screen name popped up. But his typed request surprised her.

Lena. I want to chat with your twin tonight.

Do you now? was Lena's typed response as she managed a wry smile, after regaining her composure.

Yes.

Why?

I'd like to get to know her.

Don't think that's a good idea.

Let me be the judge of that. Trust me.

Lena leaned back against her headboard trying to remember the last time she had put her complete trust in a man. When she remembered, her chin firmed as she thought stubbornly, why should she trust Morgan? But then, another part of her wanted to trust him. "I'm a big girl," she murmured softly to herself. "Maybe it's time I act like it."

Smiling, a naughty and wicked shiver sliding down her spine, she began typing. *Okay, I trust you and for the rest of the time you're online, you'll be chatting with my twin.*

Okay. Thanks for trusting me.

Lena nodded. She hadn't expected him to thank her for that.

So, Lena's twin. How are you?

Lena wasn't sure what came over her at that

moment. Maybe it was the idea that now she could, even if only for a short while, finally unleash her unruly inner self with a man she'd admitting to trusting. This was her chance to shed her inhibitions, stop being the good girl for a little while and walk on the wild side.

Taking a deep breath and before she could change her mind she began typing and felt an intense shiver when she sent Morgan her response.

I'm fine, Morgan, but I wish I was there with you.

Morgan was sitting at a large oak desk in his suite when he received Lena's response, and immediately he felt his body transform into hard steel, and inner fire began creeping through his bloodstream. The Lena Spears he knew, even the one he'd kissed the other day, would not have admitted such a thing.

Inhaling deeply he began typing. *And what would you do if you were?*

It didn't take long for her typed response. *I'd try things on you that I've never tried on a man before.*

Feeling hot, he undid the top button of his shirt before typing *Such as?*

Depends on where you are now. You're in your suite, right?

Yes.

In bed?

No, I'm sitting at the desk.

That's a good spot. I'd clear off that desk and spread my naked self on top of it.

Mercy! Morgan thought and immediately grabbed a sixteen-ounce bottle of chilled water and practically drained the entire thing just to cool off his heated body. The thought of Lena spread naked across this desk aroused such strong feelings within him that he had to lean back in his chair to place space between him and the desk. Imagining those voluptuous thighs exposed to his view sent a warm flood of anticipated and delicious pleasure racing through him.

Morgan? she typed. *You're still there?*

Barely. But instead of typing that single response, he stroked the keys to ask *And then what you would do?*

Whatever you want. I would become your every woman.

His every woman… Just the thought sent more heat escalating through him. He leaned forward, feeling a heated rush. He tried to remain calm, keep his composure, but it was hard, just like the rest of him.

Before he could type in a response she sent him a question. *And what's your fantasy, Morgan Steele?*

He smiled, not the least ashamed to admit what that was. He typed in his response. *Making love to you all day long and feel you climax beneath me several times. More times than either of us can count.* Then he smiled with a predatory satisfaction when she didn't respond for a while.

You sure about that? was the response she finally sent.

Positive. Now what's your fantasy?

To have you on top of me, making love to you, and I'd be grateful for a half day and at least one climax.

That powerful chemistry that she had failed to acknowledge the first night they'd met was back with a vengeance, stirring every volatile emotion within him. This was the Lena he wanted in his bed, and once he got her there he was going to prove they were one and the same. There weren't two sides of Lena Spears, and he planned to make sure she realized that.

Don't settle for one climax. Get ready for several, he typed and then added *Your wish will be my every command, Lena Spears. Whatever you want done, I will do...with pleasure.*

There was a pause and then she responded. *I think it's time we ended this conversation before the screens burn out.*

If we must.

We must, and remember, Morgan, tonight you chatted with the twin.

He lifted a challenging brow. The sexual excitement she had aroused in him had gotten to an intense level, had become a momentous force. There was no way he would let her cunningly fall back to being her old self. Even over cyberspace he sensed her emotional withdrawal.

Good night, Morgan.

Good night, Lena.

He waited for her to log off before he did likewise. Then he sagged back against the chair thinking he couldn't return to Charlotte quick enough to suit him.

Chapter 10

The following day Morgan discovered that he had a hard time focusing his attention on anything, even this meeting with Cameron and Ben. By the end of the day business negotiations were behind them, everything had been finalized and it was agreed that they would enter into a partnership for the development of urban real estate, with the objective of fostering economic opportunities in the underserved urban areas around the country.

Ben had caught a flight back to Los Angeles as soon as the meeting was over, and if it hadn't been for the promise Morgan had made to Cameron a few days ago to stick around and play a few rounds of golf, he would have been on the next plane bound for Charlotte. Now with the golfing behind them they both had plans to fly home on Thursday instead of Friday.

After enjoying a scrumptious meal at a very popular soul food restaurant in St. Louis, they decided to have a couple of beers while a jazz band performed.

"So how's Vanessa?"

Morgan lifted his gaze from studying the contents of his glass of beer and glanced across the table at Cameron. He smiled over at his friend. "She's no different than she was the last time you asked me about her. What can I say? Vanessa is Vanessa."

Cameron took a sip of his own beer, straight from the bottle. "Maybe it's time for me to pay you a visit in Charlotte."

Morgan chuckled. "Yeah, maybe it is. That should really shake things up a bit."

Cameron grinned. "I imagine it would. So how is the sale of your house coming?"

Cameron's questions made Morgan think of Lena, not that he hadn't been thinking about her anyway. "Lena has found several interested buyers, and I actually like the new place she found for me."

Cameron lifted a brow. "But I thought you hiring her as a real estate agent was a cunning ploy to spend time with her."

Morgan smiled. "It started out that way, but this might be one of those situations where I got caught in my own trap."

Cameron chuckled. "That doesn't bother you?"

"No, whatever works I'm for it." Moments later Morgan asked, "Why are we drawn to difficult women?"

Cameron shrugged massive shoulders as he glanced at his watch. "Because we're strong men. Any weaker man would have given up by now. Rejection is something a lot of men don't take very well. But you know that saying about only the strong surviving. I think it has become our slogan. Besides," he said, after another sip of his beer, "it's more than our nature, Morgan. It's our destiny."

Morgan's mouth formed into a determined smile. Cameron had spoken of strength, but Morgan hadn't felt strong after talking with Lena last night. In fact for a long while after their conversation he had sat in the chair behind the desk, too weak in the knees to even move. Never had he gotten so turned on from exchanging words with a woman through cyberspace. And every time he moved around in his hotel room and glanced over at his desk, he could picture a naked Lena spread on it.

He glanced over at Cameron. "So can I expect a visit from you sometime later this month?"

Cameron smiled. "Yes, that's something you can pretty much bank on."

Lena found that her emotional side was the pits. She had asked herself a million times upon wakening that morning, how had she done what she did last night? Sheesh! She could blame it on her fictional twin all she wanted, but it was her fingers that had typed in those outlandish words.

What did Morgan think of her? From his typed responses it didn't appear that he'd been put off by her behavior. In fact he seemed to have enjoyed chatting with her naughty twin. She sighed thinking that he was due back in town on Sunday and she was supposed to give him an answer to his proposal. She was no closer to making a decision than she had been the day he'd made it.

She had planned to go by his house that day to clean up any more chocolate handprints left by that little boy, but hadn't had the desire to do so. The last place she needed to go today was the place where Morgan slept, ate, bathed, dressed...

She tossed a file on her desk wondering at what point she would stop fantasizing about the man. Hadn't doing so got her in enough trouble already?

She almost jumped when her intercom sounded. Leaning forward she pushed the button. "Yes, Wendy?"

"Cassandra Tisdale is here to see you."

Lena lifted a brow. Cassandra Tisdale? What would the woman want with her? There was only one way to find out. "Send her in, Wendy."

Lena stood just moments before her office door opened and Cassandra breezed in, bringing all her air of phoniness with her. She decided not to waste any time in asking, "Cassandra, what can I do for you?"

Cassandra smiled brightly. "I think I owe you an apology."

Lena crossed her arms over her chest and eyed the woman skeptically. "Do you?"

"Yes, silly me. When I saw you and Morgan together a couple of weeks ago I jumped to the wrong conclusions when I should have known better. I just heard at lunch that you're selling his home for him. I should have known it was something to do with business and not anything personal."

Lena silently heard what Cassandra was not saying. "And why should you have known that?"

Cassandra smiled affectionately. Lena surmised that it was the same way she would have smiled at a puppy before kicking it. "Because you aren't Morgan's type. In fact I know the perfect woman for him."

Lena leaned her hips against her desk. "Do you?"

"Yes, my cousin Jamie. You probably remember her from the ball that night."

Now it was Lena who smiled. "Oh yes. Isn't that the same cousin you tried pushing off on Chance?"

Cassandra frowned. "Chance disappointed me. I always thought he appreciated the finer things in life."

"He does. That's why he married Kylie. In fact I think he's a man who recognizes top quality when he sees it."

Cassandra's frown deepened. "Well, I wish them the best. But getting back to Morgan."

"And your cousin?"

"Yes. Did you know she was his date at the governor's inaugural ball last year?"

Lena smiled. She had heard it a different way

from Kylie. It seemed the young woman was in attendance and had asked Morgan to take her home when she began not feeling well. "And?"

"And I thought he was rather taken with her."

"Really?"

Cassandra smiled. "Yes. Money marries money. What can I say?"

Nothing, Lena thought. The woman had basically said it all. Now it was her time to speak, and what she had to say would definitely burst the woman's bubble. Maybe it was the fact that she was sick and tired of the Cassandras and Jamies of the world who thought good things should happen only to them because they were born with silver spoons in their mouths, or perhaps it was because Cassandra, as usual, had rubbed her the wrong way.

Whatever the reason, Lena had had enough. "I hate to disappoint you and your cousin, but when Morgan returns to town we'll be announcing our engagement."

Cassandra blinked and then burst out laughing. "If you think Morgan is going to marry you, then you are a fool. Everyone knows he wants the perfect woman, and trust me you're far from perfect. Your lack of pedigree, your appearance, your profession. You are definitely not what

Morgan Steele needs in a wife, so if he asked you to marry him it had to be during a weak moment when he wasn't thinking rationally. Men marry women they will be proud to be seen with. Although I really don't care for Kylie or that woman Bas married, I have to admit they look decent enough. I can't say the same for you."

Anger tore through Lena and she came close to slapping that smile off Cassandra Tisdale's face, but she wouldn't let the woman know how much her words bothered her. Instead she said, "Thanks for dropping by, Cassandra, and unless you have a house you want me to sell or you're looking to buy one, I really have work to do, so please leave."

"Less than a month."

Lena raised a brow. "Excuse me?"

Cassandra tilted her head back and gave Lena a haughty look. "Jamie has moved here, and like I said, she and Morgan have dated before and if I recall they got rather cozy. I bet that, engaged or not, in less than a month she'll have Morgan and you won't."

And then she turned and breezed out of the office with the same air of phoniness that she'd breezed in with.

* * *

"What a witch," Jocelyn Steele said, putting down her cup of tea. "I can't believe Bas could have been engaged to marry such a creature."

Jocelyn had joined Kylie and Lena for lunch and Lena told them about Cassandra Tisdale's visit.

"Honestly," Kylie said, sipping her tea. "I think the brothers knew Bas would come to his senses before the wedding. Chance even told me such. And he was right. When we got back from our honeymoon we found out that Bas had broken the engagement."

"Well, I'm glad I'm the woman he chose," Jocelyn said, smiling. She then turned her attention to Lena and smiled. "So, are you and Morgan really getting married?"

Lena wanted to hold her head down in frustration. She hadn't told Morgan of her decision, but she hadn't wasted any time throwing it in Cassandra's face in anger. "I never gave Morgan an answer. I'm supposed to tell him what I've decided when he returns."

"Well, you might as well have told the entire town," Kylie said, grinning. "I bet it will be spread all over Charlotte by morning. And I hope you don't believe that garbage Cassandra said about her cousin being able to turn Morgan's head in less than a month."

Lena sighed. She had seen Cassandra's cousin and had to admit the woman was a beauty. How would Morgan react if the woman did turn her attention his way?

"Don't think it, Lena."

Lena lifted her head and met Kylie's gaze. "Don't think what?"

"That anything Cassandra said is true. Morgan is not the type of man who would be interested in a woman like Jamie Hollis. I told you what really happened that night at the governor's ball. She claimed a headache and asked Morgan to take her home."

"They've dated before," Jocelyn said.

"But still," Lena said softly, "Jamie Hollis is pretty, she's a socialite, her father is a senator, she comes from money..."

"Evidently none of those things matter to Morgan, Lena. He's made his choice," Kylie interjected. "And as far as I'm concerned you'll be bringing far more to the table, something that Morgan admires. Genuineness. You're not superficial. What people see is what they get. I personally think that's the best quality of all."

* * *

Later that night before getting into bed Lena decided she needed to call Morgan. She preferred that he hear about her conversation with Cassandra from her than from someone else. She braced herself when she began dialing his cell phone.

"Hello."

The greeting was whispered huskily and sent sensuous chills through her body. "Morgan, this is Lena."

"I know."

She raised a brow. "You do? How?"

"Caller ID."

"Oh." She rolled her eyes, calling herself a ninny for not figuring that out.

"How are you doing, Lena?"

She cleared her throat. "I'm fine. What about you?"

"I'm doing okay. How's your mom?"

"She's doing fine. Thanks for asking." Then without missing a beat she said, "Morgan, there's something I need to tell you."

"Yes?"

"About your proposal?"

"What about it?"

"Something happened today that I think you should know about."

"All right, what happened?"

Lena decided to lie back on the bed. "Cassandra Tisdale dropped by my office today and…"

"And what?"

Lena sighed. "She said some things that really rubbed me the wrong way, and before I could catch myself I told her that you and I would be announcing our engagement when you returned to town."

She heard Morgan's chuckle. "I'm sure that shut her up."

Lena shook her head. "Not quite." But Lena had no intention of telling him what else Cassandra had said, especially the part about her cousin Jamie. Instead she added, "I have a feeling it did just the opposite. I bet she's spreading it all around town now and I thought you should know."

"Okay, thanks for telling me."

"You don't sound bothered by it."

"By what?"

Lena stared up at the ceiling. "By what I told her."

"I'm not. I asked you to marry me. You just hadn't given me your answer. Does this mean you'll be accepting the terms of my proposal, Lena?"

She ran a hand over her face. "What do you want, Morgan?"

"You know what I want. I want you. I want you to have my baby. I want us to get married and be best friends. I want your mother to be an integrated part of our lives. I guess you can say I want it all."

Everything but love, she thought, tucking a stray strand of hair behind her ear. In all their conversations he never had mentioned love. She forced that thought from her mind. There were times in life when you couldn't get everything you wanted.

"Well, I'll let you go now. I just wanted you to know," she said softly.

"Okay, we'll talk more about it when I return to Charlotte."

"All right. Good night, Morgan."

"Good night, Lena."

Morgan didn't release the phone until he heard the click of Lena's disconnecting the line. Although he was overjoyed that she had decided to accept his proposal, he was curious as to what had driven her to make that decision. He couldn't help wondering exactly what Cassandra had said to her.

Morgan was astute enough to know that there

was more to the story than Lena had told him. He knew of only two people who could possibly know. Kylie was one, but when it came to Lena she had a tendency to be tight-lipped. The other person was Donovan. Donovan usually hung around in the right circles, and if there was something amiss he would be the one to know it.

He quickly keyed in Donovan's number, and his brother picked up on the first ring. "Yes?"

"Okay, Donovan, what's going on?"

He heard his brother's chuckle before he said, "You tell me. Rumor has it that you're about to become an engaged man."

Morgan smiled. So word was out already. "Yes, that's right."

"Congratulations. It seemed you got the woman you wanted. I'm not going to ask how you managed and maybe it's best if I don't know. But I better tell you the masses are taking bets."

Morgan frowned. "Bets?"

Donovan chuckled again. "Yes. It seems a certain part of Charlotte's elite society group can't imagine you and Lena as a couple. In fact they're taking bets that before it's over you'll come to your senses and marry a woman they feel is more suitable to your breeding."

Morgan's frown deepened. "And who's that supposed to be?"

"Jamie Hollis. It's my understanding Cassandra is certain her cousin can replace Lena. I understand she's even bold enough to tell Lena that."

"Oh, I see." *Now he really did.* So that's what had pushed Lena into action. He shook his head. He would take Lena over Jamie any day. And he intended to do that very thing.

"It appears that all those times you've stated you were looking for the perfect woman, everyone was forming their own opinions as to what you wanted."

Morgan sighed. "Evidently. Seems like I have a lot to straighten out when I return to Charlotte tomorrow."

"I would have to agree. You know Cassandra and her better-than-thou group."

Yes, he did know Cassandra and her group. He would have thought her broken engagement with Bas would keep her quiet for a while. Evidently now that she had returned to town she was trying to take the spotlight off her and place it on someone else.

"And before you come back to town to roll any heads, I need to remind you of something," Donovan said, breaking into his thoughts.

"What?"

"If you're still thinking about running for public office I wouldn't have my name linked to any negative publicity by stirring up trouble. You know the woman you intend to marry. I wouldn't worry about what is being said."

Morgan frowned. "I will worry about it if it involves Lena," he said roughly. "I won't have people assuming she's competing against Jamie for my attention, because she's not."

"Then show it in other ways. You know what they say about action speaking louder than words. Besides, once it's officially announced that you're engaged to Lena, if Jamie has any class she will bow out of the picture and put an end to this foolishness that Cassandra has started."

Moments later Morgan hung up the phone. All he had to do was show back up in Charlotte and put this foolishness to rest by announcing his engagement. He knew what woman he wanted and it wasn't Jamie Hollis.

Chapter 11

It occurred to Lena during lunchtime the following day that she hadn't made a pit stop by Morgan's house to clean up those chocolate smudges.

After talking to him on the phone last night and telling him what to expect when he returned she had immediately felt a sense of relief. But upon waking this morning a lot of doubt now filled her mind. Had she really made the right decision? Had she allowed Cassandra's words to push her into a situation she shouldn't really be in?

Morgan made it seem like a "marriage of

purpose" was nothing new, and maybe it wasn't to celebrities, high profilers and those Hollywood types. But she was someone who dealt with reality and she didn't know of any woman in her inner circle who would agree to marry a man and have his baby as part of a business deal. The media would have a field day with that bit of news if they ever got wind of it. And what would his brothers think? His parents? His own friends?

Not knowing what to think herself, Lena brought her car to a stop after pulling into Morgan's driveway. Unsnapping her seat belt she got out and proceeded to check his mailbox before getting the door key from the lockbox. The least she could do was bring in any mail since it seemed the box was overflowing.

Moments later she was walking inside his foyer and closing the door behind her. She smiled as she glanced around, distinctively remembering the first time he'd brought her here for that tour. And each time she had returned to his home she couldn't help but think how massive it was for one person. But then, the one he was thinking of buying was just as huge. And now that she'd decided to accept the terms of his proposal, that meant she and her mother would be sharing with him whatever house he purchased.

There were a number of framed portraits that hung on the walls, detailing the vast extent of his valuable art collection. She thought, and not for the first time, that his house smelled like him, a robust scent of man.

Walking into the living room she placed Morgan's mail on the table in a spot where he would be able to see it when he returned on Sunday. After taking off her jacket and slipping out of her shoes, she noticed a chocolate smudge on the door handle of the French door leading out to the pool and so she walked into the kitchen to get a wet cloth. She hoped and prayed there weren't too many others.

Standing at the kitchen sink she bit back a smile. One of Ms. Emily's daughters had called a couple of nights ago saying she planned to take their mother out to dinner and a movie for her birthday and had invited Odessa along. At first Lena had had mixed emotions about her mother going, but after talking to Cora Jessup and seeing how excited Odessa had gotten with the invitation, she had agreed. Hopefully, this would be the start of some sort of social life for her mother.

"You certainly have a way of brightening up my kitchen."

Lena spun around, holding a hand to her chest, as her gaze connected to Morgan's. And speaking of chest…his was broad, hairy, well defined and at the moment, naked. In fact it was obvious he had just stepped out of the shower. The only thing covering the bottom half of his body was a velour towel and it wasn't all that thick. From the look and shape of things, it was obvious he worked out regularly, which was something she herself had begun doing but not with as much zeal and dedication as some people. But she was determined to get there.

She cleared her throat after her racing heart slowed down a bit. "When did you get back?" she askcd, after she was finally able to speak. The fact that he was standing in the middle of the room looking sexy as hell was making her skin feel heated.

He cracked a gorgeous smile. "About an hour ago."

"B-but I talked to you last night. Why didn't you tell me you were coming back today?"

Striding toward her with a smile so hot it could melt butter, he said, "I wanted to surprise you."

Well, he had certainly succeeded in doing that. She tried averting her gaze from that smile only to have it fall on his chest, and she quickly decided that wasn't good. And if she moved it lower it would hit another spot. Although that area was covered, staring at it wasn't a smart idea, either. Definitely not a decent thing to do, but who could think of decency in the presence of a half-naked man?

When he came to a stop directly in front of her, pinning her between his body and the counter, she forced a smile to her lips and cleared her throat yet again before saying, "So, how was your trip?"

His smile became even sexier when he said, "Mmm, let's talk about my trip later. Right now I'd like the perfect homecoming."

And before she could blink, he leaned forward and captured her lips with his.

The moment Morgan's tongue took control of hers Lena's world turned topsy-turvy and blazing hot all at the same time. This was what spontaneous combustion was all about, she quickly decided. He hadn't given her time to react, to resist, or to think. When he had coaxed her lips apart and seized her tongue, he had been the one to take control. He was a master at what he was doing, and the sensations his skilled lips, tongue and mouth were causing shot straight to areas of her body that hadn't been touched in a long time or ever. He made the last kiss they'd shared in her office seem tame compared to this. Their tongues were mingling, tangling, mating in a private, sensual and heat-blistering dance.

She wanted to wrench her mind back from all the erratic emotions he was making her feel, all the heated lust invading her body. Instead she was being overtaken by some primal elemental force that sent vibrations of deep need all through her.

The air they were breathing seemed to change and she felt her entire body attune to that change. She heard herself moan. She felt herself surrender, and she felt herself being pulled more and more under the mastery of a Morgan Steele kiss.

Then as if that wasn't enough, his hands moved to her waist, then upward to slip beneath her blouse, unclip her bra and trace hot fingertips to caress her breasts—kneading their softness and then playing, torturing and tantalizing their taut tips. She heard herself whimper when she became entrenched in desire so strong, potent and deliberate she couldn't breathe.

It was then that he broke off the kiss. While trying to force air through their lungs their gazes held, locked, with a need that almost bordered on obsession, and she knew what he wanted. She knew what she wanted as well. Here and now.

She didn't care that they were standing in his

kitchen during midday. All that mattered, the only thing that was important, was to finish what they started. Any regrets would come later but not now. Something had taken over, held them in a sensual grip. It was something they couldn't explain, nor did they want to or feel the need to. It was enough that they both felt it. They both wanted it. And they both intended to have it.

Now.

Without uttering a word he reached out and tugged the blouse over her head, then freed the bra completely from her breasts. As he tossed both aside, his hands then moved to her hips and on bended knee he unceremoniously yanked down her skirt, leaving her standing in the middle of his kitchen wearing nothing but a thong.

"Mercy."

Lena heard his growl.

Heat drummed through her when she felt his fingers move slowly up her legs, kneading her flesh while making her body burst into flames. But it seemed it didn't intend to let her burn without him. The next thing she knew was that he was sensually stroking the back of her knee with one hand while tracing his fingertips up her inner thigh with the other. When he reached her thong, his hand slipped beneath the satin barely-there covering and touched her.

She fought the fiery sensations that single touch caused by closing her eyes, throwing her head back and pressing her knees together. She had never felt such intensity, such vulnerability, so possessed with need.

"Lena?"

Deep in the recess of her mind she heard her name. She slowly opened her eyes and looked down and met his gaze, recognizing the look in their dark depths. That look stole her breath, sent even more indescribable sensations shooting through her and made liquid heat, which she could actually feel, pool right smack between her legs where his finger still was located.

"I want you, Lena," he whispered in a husky voice, still holding her gaze. "I want you on the table."

She stared down at him. He was leaning back on his haunches staring back at her. There was a high degree of heat in his eyes, and then suddenly she felt hot all over again. He stood, laced his fingers with hers, positioned her body close to his and turned her slightly and begin inching her backward toward the table. It was then that she noticed his towel had dropped and he was as stark naked as she was.

"I've been fantasizing about you spread out on my desk, but I'm going to make this table work," he whispered huskily into her ear.

They came to a stop when the table was at her back. Morgan remembered how his brothers had joked about him having such a huge table in his kitchen. Now he knew why it was there. It was perfect. His need, his desire and his want for her had built up over a long period. She had become an obsession that nearly bordered on madness.

He wanted to marry her. He wanted her to have his baby. He wanted her to be a part of his life forever.

He *loved* her.

That stark realization ratcheted through him, nearly knocking him off balance. That was the reason why he had come up with those crazy plans, and why, even when Donovan had teased him mercilessly about Lena not giving him the time of day, he hadn't let her rejection deter him one bit from making her his priority.

He knew at that very moment that he had probably fallen in love with her the moment he set eyes on her that night, and he had dreamed about her every night since then. She had fascinated him in a way no other woman had ever done before. He saw a beauty on the outside that he knew radiated from the inside. Her dedication to her mother and those she considered friends was monumental. He admired such a high degree of loyalty and devotion. Her involvement in the various community projects around town that were geared to benefit others was a testimony that she was a person who cared. This was the type of woman he needed in his life, to walk by his side, to be there with him when the going got tough. She didn't know it yet but he had high plans for their future, and they would have a rewarding future together— she might as well bank on it.

He reached down and lifted her bottom and sat her on the edge of the table, then gently scooted her back on it. He stepped back. She was lying flat on her back with her gorgeous legs dangling off the sides, naked and opened for him. Just like he'd imagined in his fantasy.

Morgan inwardly groaned. All that naked flesh only heightened his desire. "You're beautiful, Lena," he whispered and felt the truth of his words all the way to his toes.

He watched as she slid a glance at him, smiled and said, "You have a way of making me feel sexy, Morgan Steele."

"Because you are sexy. And your sexiness has

a way of driving me wild. Pushing me over the edge and making me want to do things I normally don't do," he said truthfully.

He came back to the table, leaned over her and kissed her. Thoroughly. Deeply. And then he was between her spread knees, easing them apart even farther.

The scent of her drove him crazy, made him lose control, made his body even more aroused. He stepped closer, rubbed his hardened shaft against her wet core, teasing it, tantalizing it, provoking it in an enticing way.

"I think this is where I ask if I need to put on a condom," he whispered huskily, as he continued to rub himself against her. "As much as I want to give you my baby, now isn't the time to do it. There are too many number crunchers around here to suit me."

She smiled and slowly shook her head. "I take the pill to regulate my periods, so I'm safe, but if you prefer to—"

"No, I don't prefer. I want to be skin to skin, flesh to flesh with you. I want to know the exact moment I let go and fill you with me, Lena."

He leaned in closer to her ear, letting his warm breath touch her skin underneath when he whispered, "In other words, I want to soak your insides to the point that even next week you'll still know that I came for a visit."

And then he kissed her in a long, drugging kiss that automatically had her eyes closing while the desire within her crested, seeking fulfillment.

"Look at me, Lena," he said in a soft command after pulling back.

She opened her eyes and smiled at him. It was then that she saw that he was on the table with his body straddled over hers. The light shining through his kitchen blinds made him appear as the man he had been—her nighttime fantasy—and into the man he now was, her daytime reality. At that moment she was aware of everything. The way he was staring down at her, the way their breathing was being released in the quiet stillness of the room, the way his shaft was resting between her open legs and the sexual, hot sense they radiated.

He leaned down and placed a light kiss on the tip of her nose and smiled. "I think I'm going to keep this table forever," he said, chuckling softly. And then his expression turned serious and he leaned down and whispered, "Got to have you. Now."

He seemed to rise even higher above her before he sank back down in one fluid motion inside her.

"Oh," she gasped, her sensation one of total fulfillment and extreme gratification, knowing their bodies were connected this way. He moved deeper, going inside her to the hilt, inside her while reaching under her and bracing her voluptuous bottom, holding it tight to the fit of him.

"Does it hurt?" he asked, whispering softly against the thick luxuriousness of her hair.

"No, you feel good," she said, smiling up at him. "Okay, big guy. Show me what you can do." And with the agility of an acrobat, she lifted her legs to lock her ankles in the center of his back.

He grinned down at her. "Remember, you asked for it."

And then he began moving slow at first, easing in and out as if savoring each stroke, liking the feel of his shaft work its way inside her. And then the tempo suddenly changed, and he began pumping fast. Then faster. Relentless with need. Unbelievably detailed with each and every intimate and intense caress.

"More, Morgan. More. Don't stop," she begged.

It was on the tip of Morgan's tongue to tell her that at this point he couldn't stop even if he wanted to. So he continued to pump into her, ignoring the hard feel of her heels in the center of his back with each thrusting motion. He felt her climbing the same ladder of passion that he was climbing, knowing what awaited them at the top was one hell of an orgasm. And when she arched her back, he didn't know how it was possible but he drove deeper into her, hit something and whatever it was had her screaming her release.

He felt it, the tensing of her muscles, the pull, the clenching, and at that moment she became the epitome of everything sensual to him. She was one hell of a woman. His woman.

And then he reached the top with her, clung to everything, felt sensually trapped tight within her inner thighs, wishing he could stay a captive forever. He felt his body explode, shatter, flood her. And he bucked once, twice, a third time, appreciating the sturdiness of the table, grateful it was genuine wood and not glass. He was shattering enough. He didn't need the table to shatter as well.

He threw his head back and growled incoherently. He felt like the wolf claiming his mate and all the innate rights that came with that possession. And as his body began to slow down, he started feeling an inner peace, one he'd never felt before. He could only think of one word for what had just taken place on his kitchen table. Perfect.

He sucked in a deep breath, trying to reclaim a semblance of strength. He gazed down at her and he wanted her again. Just like that. Just like this. But the next time he wanted it in the bedroom, in the bed. This table was of good quality, but it could only take so much.

He leaned down and pressed his mouth gently to hers, not ready to separate from her. Her saw the aftermath of a sexual glaze in her eyes, watched a satisfied smile touch the corners of her lips. Grinning proudly he wanted to beat his fists against his chest. Instead he reached down and cupped her face in his hands. "Tell me," he whispered throatily. "What are you thinking?"

She grinned back at him, still trying to catch her breath. "Are you sure you want to know?"

"Yes."

"Mmm, I was just thinking that you have one hell of an organ, Morgan."

He laughed. He actually laughed and the ripples from his body went straight through to hers, making them aware they were still joined.

"Besides being a sexy lady, you're also a poet, I see."

She chuckled. "Sometimes. How about this one? *Why waste it when you can taste it?*" And then she was pulling his head down for a kiss that sent an aching need through him. When she released his mouth she smiled up at him, pleased with what she'd done.

"Arrogant woman," he teased gruffly. "You know what I think?" he asked, leaning down and brushing a kiss across her lips.

"No, what?"

"I think we should carry this discussion to the bedroom."

"Think you'll get poetic justice in there?"

"Among other things."

Lena wrapped her arms around him. "I'm curious to find out about those other things."

Chapter 12

And just to think she had convinced herself for six years that she didn't need sex, Lena thought, feeling the heated warmth of Morgan's naked body snuggled so close to hers. His even breathing was an indication that he had drifted off to sleep, but to make sure she didn't go anywhere, his arms were wrapped securely around her waist and one of his legs was thrown over hers.

They were cuddled, spoon position, in his bed after just having another round of mind-blowing lovemaking. Yes, she preferred thinking about what they'd spent doing the better part of the last two hours as making love rather than just having sex. Today he had shown her there was a difference in the two. He had been painstakingly thorough with every detail, passionate with every sensual move and personal and intimate with every word he'd whispered in her ear each and every time he entered her body.

She inhaled deeply, picking up his masculine scent while at the same time feeling an inner peace, one she hadn't felt in a long time—at least not since her father's death. Willie Spears hadn't been just a man. He had been a good father, husband and provider for "his girls," as he had often referred to her and her mother. He had been kindhearted to those he met, strong in his belief in God and a person who was always willing to lend a hand to help others. That was one of the reasons his sickness and subsequent death had taken a toll on both her and her mother.

He had requested only one promise of her, a promise she was living each day to fulfill. "Take care of my Odessa," he'd said in what had been his final hours. "Promise that no matter what, you will take care of her, Lena. She's my most precious gift that I'm leaving to you."

His most precious gift.

How many men thought of the woman they loved, when they had dedicated their lives to for so many years, as their most precious gift? And she'd always wanted to find a man just like that, someone who would think of her that way. A man whose personality, ideals and beliefs so closely mirrored her father's. She'd known that finding such a man wouldn't be easy, and for a time, while in college, she'd thought she would have to settle for less.

She wasn't exactly the type of woman that men eagerly sought out. A pleasing personality always managed to take a backseat to looks and body size. Unfortunately, Cassandra Tisdale had been right that day when she'd said that Lena wasn't Morgan's type. That only made her wonder even more why she was here, in the middle of the day in bed with him after having spent what would go down in her mind as the most memorable two hours she'd ever spent with a man. And an even more demanding question that refused to go away was why, when he could probably have any woman he wanted, he was intent on having her.

There was yet another question lurking deep in her mind. Now that he'd had her did he actually still want her? Did he still want to marry her and give her his baby? Or had she been nothing more than a puzzle he'd wanted to figure out and now that he had...

"What time do you have to pick your mom up today?"

Lena's body tensed and her fingers gripped the bedcovers when she felt Morgan's hot body edge even closer and the leg thrown across hers tighten. She'd thought he was still asleep. It had been so long, she wasn't sure how one behaved afterward. Even now she felt it, that sensual ache between her thighs that begged for more of what he had given her earlier. She felt like a downright greedy hussy, and the sad thing about it was that she could no longer blame her wanton actions on her twin.

"Lena?"

The sound of his voice, a deep, husky, sexy tone, was close to her ear, and her body instantly responded when he licked her earlobe with a hot sweep of his tongue.

"Umm?" That was the only word she could manage between flushed lips and a throat that suddenly felt tight. She felt hot and breathless.

"What time do you have to leave to pick up Odessa?" he repeated in a husky whisper that made an even deeper throb in the area between her legs.

"I don't," she managed to get out. "One of the ladies at the center who Mom became friends with is having a birthday dinner this evening and she was invited. One of the lady's daughters will be bringing Mom home later tonight. I was told not to expect her before eight."

"And do you have any more appointments scheduled for today?" was his next question.

"No."

"Good."

Before she had an indication of what he was about to do, he quickly eased himself up on his elbows and turned her toward him to stare down at her. And then he did something else she didn't expect, he tossed back the bedspread covering them, exposing their nakedness. But it wasn't his own nudity that held his attention and interest, it was hers.

His gaze left her face and slowly moved down her body, and she could actually feel the heated desire that was emanating from his eyes. She also felt his erection as it got harder and harder, pressed against the backside of her thigh. He didn't say anything, just got his fill looking.

And while he was looking at her, she was looking at him. First she began on his face, zeroing in on his lips and remembering that first kiss in her office, and the one that had started things off today in the kitchen. She still had the taste of him on her tongue.

She then moved her gaze to his throat; saw the beating of the pulse at the center before moving lower to his shoulders, then his chest. She would have arched her neck to see farther down, but then she felt his hand on her thigh and then he used those same hands to spread her knees apart.

She sighed deeply. She had discovered during the course of the last couple of hours that she had a weakness, which was turning to a raw, primal addiction, whenever Morgan's hands or fingers got close to any areas between her legs.

Like now.

There was this ache that would start right there in the center and move slowly, shivering through all parts of her body. He leaned down toward her mouth and began trailing kisses around her lips and then he pulled back, stared at her lips for a moment and then stuck out his tongue and began nibbling on her as if she was the sweetest chocolate he'd ever tasted.

Simultaneously, his fingers began going to work at her center, and she fought the tide of desire that began overtaking her. He was making her already hot body hotter. He was filling her, making the intense need within her that much greater; and he wasn't far from making her cry out in pleasure. She tried fighting it, and the more she fought it, the more she felt it. His touch was deliberate. It was precise. It was almost too much for her to handle.

"Morgan!"

He had her panting, barely breathing, and when he took his thumb and flicked it over her achy part, right in the juncture of her thighs, she felt her body teeter, right on the edge of an orgasm.

"I want to be inside you again," he whispered, easing his body in place over hers, while at the same time gently scraping his teeth against the dark skin of her shoulder.

"I want to get in and lock down," he said, lifting her hips and cupping her backside.

The only thing she could do was to release a sigh of "Oh." And the moment she did so, he swept his tongue into her mouth at the same time he eased into her body.

She gripped his shoulders. She wrapped her legs around him—not that she thought he was going anywhere. He was working it. Working her. Establishing his own rhythm, thrusting in and out. Then he flung his head back and she felt his thighs tighten, locking down on hers; felt how he clenched her hips higher to the fit of him, to go deeper inside her. She moved with him, followed his beat, his tempo, and closed her eyes thinking that this might be madness but at the moment it was madness at its finest.

It was he who screamed her name, and at that exact moment she felt his body jolt, buck, thrust continuously, almost frantically, into hers. She felt the heat of him, thick and hot, flood her insides. And then she understood what he'd meant when he'd said *lock down*. He was holding her immobile when he continued to slide in and out of her, giving her his own brand of both torture and gratification.

"Morgan!"

Then it happened to her for the umpteenth time that day. Hearing his name he cupped the back of her neck and she opened her eyes and looked at him, stared into his dark eyes, like heated chocolate chips, gazing back at her. And then without saying a word, he lowered his head and covered her mouth with his.

Lena knew at that moment she would go without a man for another six years if she thought the result would be this. Morgan Steele had definitely ended her sexual drought, and he had been well worth the wait.

And that was the last thought that crossed her mind when another orgasm hit and her body began exploding all over again.

A short while later, Morgan switched their positions to make things more comfortable for a sleeping Lena. He smiled. His perfect woman had actually fallen asleep, but that was fine. He was inside her, locked down, locked in tight and he didn't intend to go anywhere. Their legs were tangled, making them fixed in place, their bodies bolted, almost making true the words "joined at the hips." But they weren't joined at the hip. They were joined at the organs, sexual organs.

He smiled, remembering her compliment of that particular organ of his. This woman was so amazing that he couldn't think straight. All he had to do was close his eyes to remember the past several hours. He'd wanted a special homecoming but had gotten a whole lot more.

The moment he had kissed her in his kitchen he had felt it. Her response had been spontaneous, hot. And the way she had yielded to him sparked every desire within his body that could be named, arousing passions he had kept well under control for years and stirring such volatile emotions within him, he couldn't do anything but succumb to the powerful chemistry that had gripped him.

Just the thought that once they were married he would have a right to this, a chance to share a bed with her every night, had him getting hard all over again. But he had to admit what he felt was something a lot more than just physical.

He *loved* her.

Lena slowly opened her eyes and glanced around the room. When she saw it was almost dark outside she jerked up in bed and glanced over at the clock. It wasn't quite six yet.

She eased back down, released a long, ragged breath. She was alone, and for a moment that was a good thing. She needed to get her thoughts together. She closed her eyes again, and it didn't take much to remember what she and Morgan had been doing for the majority of the afternoon. She felt sore between her legs like you wouldn't believe. But that wasn't all. Her mouth felt sore as well and she couldn't help wondering if it was swollen. But each time she thought about Morgan's kisses, deep, intense, and the way he would explore her mouth, plundering it, stealing her breath away and mating almost nonstop with her tongue, she wondered just what kind of vitamins he was on.

Her nipples felt taut with her just thinking about how she responded to him, greedily taking what he was offering and then falling into peaceful sleep afterward. And when she would wake after her catnap he would be there, wide awake, with dark eyes staring down at her, focused, intent, hungry. His breathing would get shallow and she would automatically melt in a pool of succulent desire.

She heard a sound downstairs and knew that now was the perfect time to get up, get dressed and get out. The last thing she needed was for him to walk into the room while she was still in bed. If nothing else, she had discovered that when it came to Morgan Steele, she had little, if no, resistance left.

Slipping out of bed she began putting on her clothes. When she had awakened that morning she'd been a little confused, and now she was more confused than ever about just what was happening between her and Morgan.

Morgan pulled himself out of the pool after taking one last lap around it. Never in his life had he felt so rejuvenated, so bursting with energy…and so filled with love.

Now he fully understood how Chance and Bas felt. He clearly comprehended those possessive stares they would give their wives, and realized why on those days they would rush home from the office or show up late from lunch with twisted ties around their necks and silly grins on their faces.

He now had a firm handle on what emotions his two older brothers were dealing with. Hell, the only reason he had finally left Lena asleep to come downstairs for a swim was that, had he been in bed when she'd awakened, he would have been tempted to make love to her again.

Tempted, hell! He would have made love to her just as sure as there was a Charlotte sky overhead.

He began drying off with the huge towel, knowing that he and Lena needed to talk. They needed to announce their intentions to marry to their families and to anyone else who wanted to listen. He was ready to go to the tallest building and begin shouting.

"I'm leaving now, Morgan."

He turned and saw her standing in the doorway that separated his family room from his patio. Seeing her standing there, looking as sexy as sexy could get, and remembering what they had shared most of the afternoon sent a shiver of deep desire combined with hot excitement through him.

He tossed aside the towel and began walking toward her. When he got within three feet of her he noticed the apprehension in her eyes, the uncertainty, and he wondered, how could she not know, not sense how he felt at that moment? But then he had to admit they hadn't had a normal relationship. He had been a man with a plan, first using business and then ultimate pleasure to seduce her, win her over. But he had a feeling he hadn't completely won her over. She was having doubts, and from the look in her eyes, lots of them.

He could get on bended knee and tell her to hell with that business proposal. He wanted to marry her because he loved her. But would she believe him? He doubted it. Lena was a woman who would need more action than words, and that's just what he would give her. By the time she walked down the aisle to him, there would be no doubt in her mind just how deep his emotions were for her.

Instead of saying anything when he reached her, he took hold of her hand and gently pulled her closer to him. Then he leaned down and gently touched his lips to hers. He pulled back, cupped her jaw and intently studied her lips. She definitely looked like a woman who'd been well kissed all afternoon.

"What are you going to tell Odessa if she asks what happened to your lips?"

Lena's shoulders shrugged, but he saw the mocking challenge in her gaze and immediately sensed some sort of withdrawal taking place. It was a withdrawal he refused to have.

"I don't know. Got any suggestions?"

He returned that look by cocking a challenging eyebrow. "You can always tell her the truth, Lena. That we got carried away today and—"

"I don't think so."

He smiled. "I figured as much. I guess you can claim you got swollen lips from sipping too long on a soda bottle."

She lifted her own brow. "Can that happen?"

He chuckled. "It happened to Donovan once, or so he claims."

She rolled her eyes. "Well, if she asks I guess that's one excuse I could try." She then glanced at her watch. "I need to go, Morgan."

"Okay, and we need to talk. Will Odessa be at the day care again tomorrow?"

"No, she'll be at home all day watching her soaps."

He nodded. "Will you have dinner with me tomorrow? We can make it early. You and I need to talk."

She inhaled deeply. Yes, they did. "Okay, what time?"

"How about four? Is that time good for you?"

"Yes, that time is fine." She turned to leave and remembered he was still holding her hand.

"Hey, not so fast," he said, looking into her eyes. Then slowly he lowered his head and kissed her, gently and deeply.

Before releasing her he whispered into her ear, "And get on your computer tonight. Around ten. I want to talk to your twin."

Sensations rushed through Lena's body as she remembered their last conversation and how they had come close to playing out that fantasy in his kitchen. But still, she wasn't certain exchanging sexual banter in cyberspace again was a good idea. "I might be busy."

"If you're not, then pop into my space."

She nodded and quickly turned and left.

Chapter 13

Odessa had been so chatty about how her day and evening had gone that if she'd noticed anything odd about Lena's lips she hadn't said anything. Despite her initial concern, by the time she had gotten home, taken a shower and eaten a salad for dinner, Lena was too keyed up to worry about how her mouth looked. Her main concern was her future.

Morgan had left her with the impression that the business deal between them was still in place, but she needed to know for certain, which is why she had readily accepted his invitation to dinner.

After getting her mother settled for the night she had slipped into a nightgown and gone into her room to read some real estate literature she'd received in the mail. She tried ignoring her laptop that was sitting on the desk in her room. And she tried not to notice the time. It was after nine. Close to nine-thirty.

Moments later she glanced at the clock again. It was ten. She sighed and glanced over at her laptop. Should she or shouldn't she? Hadn't she gotten into enough trouble with Morgan today? Okay, she would admit that after the type of afternoon she'd had it would only be natural to want to spend time talking to him again. But why not by phone instead of cyberspace?

She quickly knew the answer to that one. She and Morgan had crossed the lines of professionalism on their laptops in a way that they could never retract. And although she had claimed it was her twin being naughty and not her, her behavior this afternoon had proven differently. And on top of that, there was something relaxing and comforting, as well as daring, in having a private, intimate and provocative conversation with someone you knew, yet didn't really know at the same time.

Deciding to stop fighting the impulse, she tossed the magazine aside and got out of bed and reached for her laptop. Taking a deep breath she quickly logged on. It was almost ten minutes after the hour. Had he checked to see if she'd logged on and when he found out she hadn't had already logged off? She inhaled deeply again, knowing there was only one way to find out.

She signed on with her Internet server and sighed in relief when his name was still there. Leaning back against the headboard she settled into a comfortable position and waited. She didn't have long for action when Morgan clicked on, invading her space.

Lena?

She clicked a response. *Yes, I'm here.*

Thanks for dropping by.

And then their fun time began.

Morgan asked the first question. *What's your favorite sport?*

Lena chuckled. That would be a quick response and she typed it in. *I really don't have one.*

Umm, have you ever played Sex by Design?

She lifted a brow and her fingers went to work. *No. How is it played?*

Easy. All you need is one woman and one man.

She shook her head, grinning as she clicked a response. *Good. I don't go for that kinky stuff.*

Neither do I.

Good to know. So, how do you play it?

You think of a word, the first one that comes to your mind, and the other person has to come up with some sort of sexual story about it.

Lena frowned. *That's a lot of typing.*

Abbreviations are accepted.

Okay.

I'll let you go first and you give me a word.

She paused a moment to think hard. She glanced around the room and smiled when she saw something on her dresser and decided not to make things easy for him. *Cotton balls.*

Cotton balls?

Yes.

There was a long pause and then he began typing. *Picture this. You and me together, naked in bed. Like we were this afternoon.*

Heat shivered through her bloodstream. *Okay I got the picture.*

And I take a bunch of those little cotton balls and strategically place them to cover your front. You know, that particular area between your legs. They will fit you like a perfect triangle. Then I use my mouth to remove them, one by one. The object is not to let one fall. Each time I remove one I get to lick the area where it had been.

Lena swallowed. Her mouth suddenly felt dry, tight, and her nipples felt hard against her nightgown. She couldn't help but type and ask. *What happens when they're all gone?*

Then I get to taste the entire area; nibble and lick as much as I want. Then I get to use my mouth and place them back and start the game all over again. So what do you think?

When visions of him doing that engulfed her mind, what Lena really thought was that they had to be nuts to be having this sort of conversation, especially when the most prolific and exquisite sensations flowed through her body. *I think we've said enough for tonight.*

Chicken. Where's your twin?

Some place safe. Good night, Morgan.

Good night, Lena.

Morgan was standing at the window the next day thinking about his and Lena's cyberspace chat of the night before when his secretary's voice on the intercom intruded into this thoughts.

"Yes, Linda, what is it?"

"Edward Dunlap is here to see you."

Morgan raised a brow before saying, "Please send him in."

A few minutes later Edward walked in. He was in his late fifties, the same age as Morgan's father. In fact, his father and the man had been business associates for years before Edward had chosen a life of politics. He had been elected as Charlotte's first African American councilman and remained in that office for years. From there he had become a state representative and was now eying a position in Congress. In recent years he had appointed himself as Morgan's mentor, determined to see him enter the political arena.

"Edward, this is a surprise," Morgan said, crossing the room to shake the older man's hand.

"Yes, and I hate to come unannounced but this meeting is important. Word has it that Roger Chadwick will be holding a press conference in a few hours to announce his candidacy. So you know what this means?"

Morgan leaned back against his desk. Yes, he knew what that meant. If he was going to announce his own intentions to run for that same seat, now was the time to finally make up his mind. "Yes, I know what it means, Edward, but there is someone I need to discuss this with."

Edward nodded. "And that brings me to another

reason I'm here. There's a rumor floating around about you."

Morgan lifted a brow. "What rumor?"

"That you're thinking of getting married."

Morgan couldn't help the smile that touched his lips. "That's no rumor. I am getting married."

"I think we need to discuss that, Morgan."

"Discuss what?"

"Your choice of a wife."

Morgan cast him a glance that nearly bordered on anger. "Excuse me?"

"I said your choice of a wife. I understand you're thinking about marrying Lena Spears, which comes as a surprise because I wasn't aware you were serious about anyone."

Morgan frowned, wondering if the man assumed he had to know everything about his business, personal or otherwise. "Yes, I've asked Lena to marry me."

"I'm sure you know family name, style and connections are everything."

"To some people."

Edward shook his head. "Don't kid yourself. You're a Steele about to run for office. You don't need to consider marrying any woman who won't be an asset to your career. Lena Spears is a nice woman, but she won't do as a wife for you. Now, take Senator Hollis's daughter. I understand she's—"

"No, you take Senator Hollis's daughter," Morgan said, after having heard enough. "For God's sake, Edward, this is the twenty-first century. Lena won't be the one running for office, I will. And who I decide to marry is really no one's business."

"Don't make the mistake of thinking it's not, Morgan. I met with a few people earlier today and the rumor of your possible engagement came up. They asked that I come and meet with you to discuss it."

Morgan straightened his stance, getting angrier by the minute. "In that case, tell them you have met with me and discussed it. And that my response is that in my opinion Lena Spears has more style and beauty in her little finger than most women have in their entire body. I'm marrying her and if the masses don't like it, then I'll run without their support."

"You won't win."

Morgan chuckled. "I might not get their vote, but if they feel the way they do about the woman I intend to marry, then I don't want their vote. They only represent a small population of Charlotte's society. I refuse to believe that the majority of the people in this town is that narrowed-minded and shallow. Good day, Edward."

Edward stared at him and shook his head for a moment before turning and walking out the door.

"For Pete's sake, calm down, Morgan."

Chance, Bas and Donovan watched as an angry Morgan paced back and forth around his office. As soon as Edward had left, Morgan had summoned his brothers. After he'd told them about Edward's visit and what had been said, they had gotten just as angry as Morgan. But not quite.

"I can't believe Dunlap actually said that to you," Donovan said, shaking his head as he sat in one of the chairs in the room. "I can see him saying that to me since he never liked me anyway."

Bas rolled his eyes. "Might be from that time he caught you *almost* making out with his youngest daughter in a parked car right in front of his house."

"Hey, she asked for it," Donovan said in defense. "What was I supposed to do?"

Chance shook his head. "Turning her down might have been the decent thing to do," he said sarcastically. "But let's get back to the issue of Morgan and Lena."

Morgan stopped his pacing and met Chance's gaze. "There's no issue. Who the hell do they think they are, deciding what woman is appropriate for me?" he asked angrily. "It's nobody's business who I marry."

"Damn right it's not, now let's go kick some asses," was Bas's quick reply.

Now it was Chance who rolled his eyes. Everyone in Charlotte knew that of all the Steeles, Bas had always been the hothead, the one ready to not only start trouble but put an end to it as well. He'd always been known as the not-so-sterling Steele, a reputation he'd garnered proudly until he turned twenty-one, dropped out of college and had to face the real world...and a man by the name of Jim Mason—Jocelyn's father.

"Just think how that sounds, Bas. Fighting never solves anything. What we need to do is to put our heads together. Whether you want to admit it or not, Morgan, you're going to need Edward and his group's support."

"Then I don't want it, and in that case I won't run."

Chance shook his head. "Think hard on that before making a decision. Have you discussed any of this with Lena?"

"No."

"Don't you think you should? Especially if the two of you are getting married, which is a mystery within itself. Two weeks ago she wasn't giving you the time of day," Chance said, eying his brother curiously. "What happened?"

Morgan stared at his brothers, and since he wanted to make sure they understood the depth of his feelings for Lena he said, "Love happened. I fell for her that night of the charity ball. I just thought I wanted her. But it's more. I love her."

Chance and Bas slowly nodded, indicating they understood. They had been there, done that and were still doing it. However, it was Donovan who was looking at him with what amounted to pity in his eyes.

"Okay, then," Chance said, smiling, as if satisfied with what he'd been told. "I suggest you talk things over with Lena. I probably won't go so far as to tell her about Edward's visit, but I think she at least deserves to know you're thinking about running for a political office."

Morgan nodded, knowing Chance was right. He and Lena had a dinner date later that day. He would tell her of his decision then.

* * *

Lena glanced around. She was lucky that although she'd arrived at the restaurant early, there had been a table reserved for her.

McIntosh Steak House and Seafood was a popular restaurant in town. Simple and elegant it catered to businesspeople with money, the power brokers of Charlotte. The interior spoke of old money with its plush carpeting, the rich-looking furnishing and the expensive art collections of oil paintings on the walls. Service was always magnificent, the food always tasty. Sometimes people traveled for miles just to dine here.

The waiter had already brought her one glass of wine and had come to see if she wanted another when she glanced up and saw Cassandra Tisdale and a couple of women she recognized as being in the woman's inner circle, including her cousin Jamie. She immediately got cold chills.

She hoped they would pass by the table and not see her as they were leaving the restaurant, but it seemed that was one layer of hope that wouldn't be granted.

"Well, if it isn't the woman who thinks she's going to be the future Mrs. Morgan Steele."

Lena glanced up, smiling. She refused to let Cassandra's snide comment rattle her. "Hi, Cassandra, Debra, Karen and Jamie. I see the four of you are leaving."

"Yes, we are," Debra Kendall said, almost apologetically. And not for the umpteenth time Lena had to inwardly question why someone as nice as Debra would hang around with someone like Cassandra. Maybe she believed that sooner or later her kindness would rub off on Cassandra.

"So, what do you think of Morgan running for office?" Karen Smith asked, after looking at Cassandra and getting her cue.

"Excuse me?" Lena asked.

Cassandra smiled. "Oh, didn't you know? Now that Chadwick has announced he's running for office, speculation is high that Morgan will, too. He's very well thought of in this town."

Lena didn't say anything. She was still recovering from Karen's comment about the possibility of Morgan being a political candidate.

"Of course it's not definite whether Morgan is even interested," Debra said, as if to smooth things over.

"But if he does," Cassandra said, grinning, "he's going to need a woman who will complement him. Someone well groomed with a good name, a sense of fashion, style and grace, and a pedigree. Wouldn't you agree, Lena?"

Before Lena could say anything, it was Jamie who spoke, smiling sweetly. "And I'm sure if you care anything for Morgan as well as recognize what an asset he would be in this community in politics, then you'd agree that all of us need to give him all the support he needs and the chance to win. I understand entering politics has been his lifelong dream. If you really care for him, you wouldn't take that dream away. In fact you would work hard to make it become a reality."

Then three of the women walked off. Debra, however, remained behind long enough to at least say goodbye.

The cold chills Lena had gotten earlier were there in full force. Why hadn't Morgan mentioned he was thinking about entering politics? Did he just assume she would want to be a politician's wife? Well, she didn't. She was a person who liked her life the way it was. She and her mother lived a quiet and peaceful existence, and she had no intention of being thrust out into the limelight.

Besides, how much did Morgan know about her? Oh, he'd learned a lot about her this afternoon and probably from the two chats they'd had, but that had all been sexual. What did Morgan really know about her? Nothing. If he did, he would know that she and politics didn't mix because she was too opinionated when it came to certain issues and she didn't know how to remain quiet when it involved a subject she was passionate about.

She thought about what Cassandra and her group said as well as what they didn't say. The people she hung out with, as well as those her parents hung out with, had a lot of influence and power. They would back Morgan fully if he had what they perceived as the right kind of wife by his side. But she knew they wouldn't use any of that to help get him elected if he was intent on marrying her.

Her father had once told her there was more to be an elected official than working on balancing the budget, attending meetings and making speeches. There was a matter of respect and Morgan had it, from a lot of people; but it seemed he ran the risk of losing it because of her, mainly because she was not a fit.

She paused and sat quietly for a moment, and when she felt a tear slide from her eye to wet her cheek, she knew why. At some point during their business relationship, those sexy chats and their romp between the sheets yesterday, she had fallen in love with Morgan. And she had fallen hard. So hard that she knew what she had to do. She could only think of one other time she'd actually felt noble in her life. The first had been at thirteen when she'd actually saved Paula Brewster's baby sister from drowning in the community pool, and the other time was now.

To help Morgan retain his regal public image and give him all the support he needed to pursue what evidently was his lifelong dream, she knew what she had to do. Summoning the waiter over to the table she said, "Please bring me my check, and when Mr. Steele arrives let him know something came up and I had to leave."

Chapter 14

Not ready to go home yet, Lena returned to her office. She had placed a quick call to her mother to make sure she was okay and had eaten dinner. After Odessa had assured her that she was fine and not to worry about her, Lena decided to stay and work late at the office.

Wendy had already left for the day and the office was quiet. Although Lena tried concentrating on the listing of new homes she had in front of her, she found her focus wasn't what it should be. One part of her was absorbed with anger for a certain group of people—those who thought they were influential enough to dictate how people should live their lives and with whom. Then another part of her knew that bowing out was the best thing. It had nothing to do with pride, confidence or self-esteem but everything to do with making a sacrifice for the man she loved. Under any other circumstances, she and Morgan might have had a chance to make their "marriage of purpose" work, but now entering into such an agreement with him would serve no purpose. He needed a different type of woman to be by his side and have his baby, and that woman wasn't her.

She glanced up when the phone on her desk began to ring. She picked it up. "Yes?"

"It's Morgan."

Lena's throat suddenly felt tight. She swallowed past the lump before saying, "Yes, Morgan?"

"I'm outside at your office door. Let me in."

When she heard the click she pulled the phone away from her ear and stared at it a few moments before hanging it up. The last person she wanted to see right now was Morgan. She rubbed the bridge of her nose and slumped back in her chair. If he had given her time, she would have told him to go away because she couldn't see him now.

Not bothering to slip back into her shoes she stood and headed down the hallway toward the door. She could clearly see Morgan through the glass front. As usual, he was dressed immaculately like the businessman he was. He was wearing a navy blue suit, a light blue shirt and a printed tie that coordinated perfectly.

She turned off the alarm and unlocked the door and then stepped back as he entered and watched as he raised a brow and searched her face. "Are you okay?"

She wondered if he'd found out about her conversation with Cassandra and her nasty-girl squad but then figured that he couldn't have. "Yes, I'm fine. Why wouldn't I be?"

He crossed his arms over his chest and stared at her. "You tell me. We had a dinner date and when I arrived one of the waiters said you had been there but left, and that you'd left a message that something had come up and you had to leave. Of course the first thought that crossed my mind was that something had happened to Odessa. I tried calling you at home and she picked up. When I asked for you she said you were at the office working late. So what was the big emergency, Lena?"

If only he knew. But at the moment she didn't

plan on telling him anything. "There was no big emergency, Morgan. I figured there were some things I could be doing here and figured our talk could wait. No biggie."

He continued to stare at her and then gestured to the hallway leading to her office. "Do what you were doing before I got here while I bring everything in."

She arched a brow. "Everything like what?"

"Dinner."

"Dinner?"

"Yes, dinner," he replied. "Have you eaten?"

"No, but I didn't expect you to bring me anything."

"No, what I expected was to have dinner with you at McIntosh's. So I got takeouts."

Her brows arched a little higher. "*McIntosh* doesn't do takeouts."

"They do if you know the right people."

At the moment that wasn't what she needed to hear. She threw up her hands. "Yes, you're right," she all but snapped. "It's all about connections, isn't it?"

He frowned. "What do you mean by that?"

"Nothing," she said and quickly turned away from him. After taking a deep breath she turned back toward him. "I'm just not in a good mood at the moment."

He nodded as if he understood when he honestly didn't have a clue, she thought. "Look, I have a tray table around here somewhere. I'll go dig it out." And then she walked off, leaving him standing there.

By the time Lena had located the tray table, Morgan had brought in all the bags of food, and a delicious scent filled her office. If she wasn't hungry before, she was certainly hungry now. She also noticed that Morgan had brought in his briefcase.

"Need help with anything?" he asked.

She glanced over in his direction. He had removed his jacket and looked rather comfortable in her office. "No, I don't need help. Thanks for asking."

"No problem."

She continued what she was doing as she drew in a deep breath. She and Morgan were virtually acting like strangers and not like the two people who had mated like rabbits yesterday. A part of her wished she could remove what happened yesterday from her mind. And then there was the chat they'd had online last night. How can you move from a high level of intimacy to a lower one that was basically nonintimate?

"Now that does it. I set you up over here," she

said, after placing a tray table near the sofa. "And I'll just use my desk."

She met his gaze, and the smile that touched his lips let her know he'd caught on to what she'd done. She had deliberately placed him away to the other side of the room. "Any reason I can't share your desk with you?" he asked, with eyes that glinted with mischief.

She shrugged as she moved toward her desk. "I thought you'd want more room."

"What I really want, Lena, is more of you."

She quickly turned back toward him and paused to take a deep, calming breath. His words hadn't been what she'd expected. And the impact they had on her was unnerving. The sexual excitement, desire and longing that she'd tried not to think about were now hitting her in the face. She felt her heart as it began to race and her stomach began fluttering.

Before she could say anything he said, "But I'll behave and stay on this side of the room...for now."

She glared at him and started to say something, but then changed her mind and crossed the room to her desk.

Once Lena had settled in at her desk and begun eating, the mischief that had been in Morgan's eyes a few moments ago was replaced with concern. Something was going on with Lena and he couldn't help wondering what. Had she heard anything about the possibility of him going into politics? Even if she had, why would that have driven her to cancel their dinner date and leave the restaurant before he had arrived?

And from the moment he had walked into her office, he had sensed her withdrawal. She was definitely not acting like the woman who had shared his bed for almost four hours yesterday. He didn't know what was bothering her, but he was determined to find out, and whatever it was, he intended to remove it from between them.

He settled on the sofa and placed the tray table in front of him and unloaded the bag with his food. He glanced over at her. She was eating, not saying anything, so he decided to break the silence. "I dropped by your house and left your mom something to eat as well."

He watched as she quickly lifted her head and a surprised look was on her face. "You did?"

"Yes. She said she'd already eaten but would save it as leftovers for tomorrow."

Lena nodded. "Thanks. That was thoughtful of you, Morgan."

"You're welcome." He watched as she took another sip of the iced tea that had been included with her dinner. When her lips touched the edge of the cup his stomach clenched, as he remembered how his lips had devoured hers yesterday, which then reminded him of something else.

"Did your mom ask why your lips were bruised when she saw you last night?"

Lena lifted her head and their gazes connected. "No, she didn't ask," she responded softly. "Why?"

"Just curious." And what he didn't add was that asking her about it would make her remember, just in case she had forgotten.

"Everything tastes good, Morgan. Thanks again for thinking of me."

"I always think of you, Lena."

Heat. Awesome heat, vibrant heat flowed all through Lena. It wasn't what he'd said but rather how he'd said it. And she wondered if this was a game he was playing with her. And had yesterday been a game as well? She inhaled deeply. No matter what, she refused to let Morgan get next to her until he was totally up front with her. Then she would be up front with him and let him know their deal was off. She was not the woman he needed to move his career forward.

For the next few moments they continued to eat in silence, sharing little or no conversation. But each time she would glance over at him, he would be watching her with an intensity that made it almost impossible to chew her food. He could generate so much heat within her from just a look, and she could feel even more heat radiating from the depths of his eyes each time he looked at her.

So she tried not to look over at him, but she still felt it. The chemistry, the attraction and the desire that wouldn't go away no matter how hard she was fighting it.

"Would you like some dessert?"

She raised her head and met his gaze. "What?"

He smiled. "Dessert. I think they put everything in my bag. I bought slices of chocolate cake."

"No, thanks. I'm full. I'll just save it for tomorrow."

He nodded and then stood. "Okay. I'll start discarding the trash. Do you have a Dumpster nearby?"

"Yes. It's out back."

She watched as he began putting everything back in the bags. He had rolled his sleeves up and she couldn't help but notice all the hair on his arms. But then, she'd noticed yesterday just what a hairy man he was. He had hair all over—his chest, his thighs and even that thick thatch where his manhood rested.

"You're through?"

She looked at him. He was standing in front of her desk. "Excuse me?"

He chuckled. "I asked if you were through. All the food is gone off your plate, but you're still sitting there, holding your fork like you're going to take another bite where there's nothing left."

"Oh," she said and immediately dropped the fork down on her plate. "Sorry, I was just thinking about something."

"No problem. I've been sitting over there thinking about some things as well."

She lifted a brow. "You have?"

"Yes. It seems my mind has been busy a lot lately."

She nodded. His mind wasn't the only thing that had been busy a lot. He had used his mouth and hands yesterday with a skill that was absolutely astounding.

"I'm taking the trash out. I'll be back in a second."

"All right." It was only when he left the room that she finally let out a deep sigh. She couldn't help wondering what was next. Would he be leaving when he returned or would he be staying? And if he stayed what did he intend to do?

* * *

He didn't leave, nor did it seem he intended to. When he returned she had deliberately placed work on her desk to look busy. He had merely crossed the room, folded up the tray table and then sat down with his briefcase. She started to ask what he was doing but it had been obvious. He'd evidently brought work with him to do and intended doing his while she did hers.

For the next half hour or so, the only sounds that could be heard in the room was their breathing and papers shuffling. But there was something comforting, relaxing and intimate about them sharing space that wasn't cyberspace.

He finished working on whatever papers he had long before she did and stood, stretching his muscles before walking over to the window. Her office was located in one of those minimalls that faced a busy street. When Morgan opened one of the blinds, she saw that the parking area was pretty well lit and already the floodlights had come on and it wasn't even six o'clock yet.

She knew Morgan was standing there, studying the casual surroundings out the window. She, however, was studying him. Her gaze flowed across the contours of his back that was covered with his dress shirt, remembering how she had placed love bites on that back yesterday. At the time she'd thought they were merely nibbles, but now, considering how she felt about him, she knew they'd been love bites.

And then there were his slacks, the way they fit his thighs and hips, and the way he had his hands shoved into his pockets showed just what a fine tush he had. She decided she had read enough and placed her papers aside. More memories of yesterday filled her mind, and suddenly that ache between her thighs returned. On top of that, her body began humming with awareness, and it became charged as if certain parts of her had lives of their own.

She tried fighting the feelings. What she and Morgan needed to do was to talk. He needed to tell her about his decision to get into politics, and she needed to explain to him why it wouldn't work between them. The last thing she should be doing was sitting there ogling him and inhaling his scent, remembering his taste and the very feel of him buried deep within her.

Hard Steele.

She blinked when he suddenly turned and caught her staring. The depths of the dark eyes gazing back at her caused a hot flame to burst to life within her. If nothing else they had proven yesterday that when it came to the sexual chemistry between them they had a tendency to act on it, regardless of the time or the place.

And she had a feeling tonight would be one of those times.

She could feel it. It was there in the air again, transmitting between them like hot lava. It was like a heated mist, surrounding them in a sexual haze. Instinctively she pushed back her chair and stood. No matter if they were on the verge of going separate ways, there was no way she could let tonight end without feeling the hardness of him embedded within her one last time.

Through eyes filled with desire she watched as he closed the blinds and pulled his shirt from within his pants and began unbuttoning it. When he had completely removed it and tossed it aside, her body responded. This was the naked chest that had rubbed against her bare breasts yesterday. The chest she had covered with more kisses than she could count.

She walked from around her desk but stayed a good distance from him. "I feel hot," she said, her voice breathy and husky in a way it could get only around him.

"Then let me cool you off," was his reply.

"Cool me off or make me hotter?"

He only shook his head and smiled before saying, "I'll let you be the judge."

Emboldened by the same force that had overtaken her yesterday, she began removing her blouse while he watched her. His gaze was intense, intimate and hot. After tossing her blouse aside she unsnapped her bra. Her breasts poured out before she could get the bra off completely and she felt a sheen of perspiration forming between the twin globes.

She shimmied out of her skirt and when she stood in front of him wearing a thong, this one black lace and covering less of her femininity than the one she'd worn yesterday, he suddenly made a sound. She heard the low growl that radiated from deep within his throat. It was then that he moved away from the window to return to the sofa and sat down and continued to hold her gaze. And then in a deep, husky, desire-laden voice, he said, "Come here, Lena."

On legs that could barely hold her, she slowly crossed the room to him, locked with a gaze that was so intense it nearly took her breath away. When she came to a stop between his widened thighs, he leaned forward, almost bringing him face-to-face with her womanly core.

His face was so close she could feel his breath through the thin wispy material. And then she felt something else, the wetness of his tongue as he snaked it out and began licking the lace. She remembered their chat the night before, and suddenly she felt so weak she had to reach out and grab hold of his shoulders to keep from falling.

Then he was pushing her a few steps back so that he could ease down on his knees in front of her.

"I need to taste you, Lena," he whispered in a husky voice, still holding her gaze.

His words torched the flame within her, suddenly made her crazy with desire. She watched his breathing quicken, his eyes darken just mere seconds before he lowered his head and began kissing and licking his way upward, toward her inner thigh.

"Open your legs for me, baby," he requested softly and it was then she realized she still had them pressed together. The moment she opened them he slowly peeled the thong down her legs, leaving her completely bare for his view.

His finger that was lodged between her legs moved and she inhaled a sharp breath. "You're awfully wet, baby," he whispered huskily. "And I can't imagine letting all that deliciousness go to waste."

And before she could draw her next breath he was kissing and licking his way up her inner thigh again. The moment she felt his hot breath within inches of her womanly core, she dug her hands in his shoulders, bracing for the onslaught, and when it happened, when his tongue invaded her, both torturing and satisfying the ache between her legs, she almost lost consciousness. But he wouldn't let her. The sensations that tore into her were too sharp and keen. Too electrifying to do anything other than to enjoy the moment.

So she held on as he relentlessly devoured her, tonguing and sucking, as sensations shot all the way through her bloodstream. She felt the explosion and tried pushing him away before it happened, but his hand was firm, possessively cupping her hips steady, locked to his mouth as his tongue continued to pound into her over and over.

"Morgan!"

She heard herself making moaning sounds at the same exact time she felt her stomach constrict. And she began experiencing sensations that swept through her that were so strong, so totally out of her control that they had her screaming. It was like nothing she'd ever felt before. Her body began vibrating between her thighs and she found herself pushing hard against his hot mouth instead of pulling away from it.

It took some doing but the sensations began ebbing and her body was slowly being pulled back into dimension. There was a heartbeat of silence and then she heard Morgan say huskily, "Get ready, baby. We've barely got started yet."

Chapter 15

Lena glanced across the room at the man who was putting back on his clothes while she put back on hers. "We never got around to talking," she said, forcing herself to speak calmly.

There hadn't been anything remotely calm about what she and Morgan had shared for the past hour. Even now she knew they weren't through with each other. It was bad enough they couldn't get dressed without looking at each other, but there was this surge of nonstop desire that kept flowing through her.

"I know. Do you need to call your mother and check on her?"

She knew why he was asking. She should have been gone hours ago. It was almost eight. She couldn't recall the last time she stayed away from home that late in the evening. "That's not a bad idea." She then tossed aside the blouse she was about to put on and walked over to her desk to call home, not missing the glint of heated desire she saw in the depths of his dark eyes.

Moments later she hung up the phone, shaking her head and chuckling. "What's so funny?" Morgan asked.

"Mom was on the other line with Ms. Emily and rushed me off."

"That's her friend from the day care, right?"

"Yes. Sounds like the two of them are having one whale of a conversation. Usually Mom is in bed by nine, but she said they would be chatting for a while tonight."

"Sounds like she's found a good friend."

Lena nodded. "Yes, it seems that way. I'm glad she's finally coming around, but she's been depressed for so long that…"

"That what?"

"Although I always wanted her to come out of it, a part of me wondered if she ever would."

Morgan nodded. He then crossed the room to stand in front of her and cupped her chin, gently lifting it so their eyes could meet. "And?"

She arched a brow. "And what?"

"And how do you feel about that?"

Sometimes she felt he could read her like a book. "Of course a part of me is happy, Morgan, but then, I've gotten used to being there for her, taking care of her, and having her to need me."

He smiled. "And you'll always do that—be there for her, take care of her—and she will continue to need you."

As if he knew she needed a hug he pulled her into his arms and rested his chin on the top of her head. "But I know how you feel. I felt that way when Chance got married again."

Lena pulled back and met his gaze. "You did?"

"Yes. I would never tell Chance but Bas, Donovan and I have always looked up to him. He seemed to always make the right decisions when it concerned not only the company but us as well. My father was a strict disciplinarian. He was a good man, but strict. He and Bas butted heads more times than I care to remember, and when

Bas dropped out of college and had no contact with the family for almost a year, he did maintain contact with Chance."

Lena nodded. "But why did it bother you when Chance married?"

Morgan smiled. He knew she was asking mainly because Chance had married her best friend. "It bothered me because since Cyndi's death, he hadn't really shown any real interest in a woman until Kylie. I thought she would come and disrupt our little family circle."

"But she didn't," Lena said defensively to the point it made Morgan chuckle.

"No, she didn't. In fact I think she's the best thing for Chance and Marcus, as well as for us. And now with Bas married and Jocelyn getting ready to manage one of Cameron's construction companies here, it seems the Steele brothers are getting married one by one, although the jury is still out on Donovan, and will be for a while. He claims he's having too much fun to settle down."

Lena inhaled a deep breath knowing whether by accident or intentionally, Morgan had given her the opening she needed for them to start talking about their issues. "Morgan?"

"Yes?"

"Why didn't you tell me you were thinking of running for public office?"

For a few moments he didn't say anything, and then he released her and took a step back as if he needed full control of his mind and body to respond to her question. "I hadn't really made a decision. Before I had merely thought about it."

She nodded. "And now?"

"And now I have made a decision and will officially announce my candidacy next week."

She inhaled deeply. "When were you planning to tell me?"

"This afternoon at dinner. And then tonight, which is why I came over here. But I kind of got distracted."

They both had. She moved across the room to stand at the window. Opening the blinds she looked out. Like him she needed full control of her mind and body. After several moments she turned toward him. "I hope you know this changes everything and I can no longer agree to your business proposal."

Immediately, she felt his inner tension. "One has nothing to do with the other, Lena."

She shook her head. "Yes, it does. I'm not cut out to be a political wife."

"I think you are."

"You need someone else by your side, Morgan. Someone who would complement you and—"

He crossed the room. "What the hell are you saying?" he asked angrily. "Don't you think I'm old enough to know what I want and need?"

"Yes, but when you had made that decision things were different. Then all you needed was a woman who would have your baby. Now you need a…"

"Trophy wife?" he asked in a tone of voice filled with even more anger.

She sighed deeply. "Yes, if you want to refer to it as such."

"So me wanting you as the mother of my child means nothing?"

"It did before but not now." Lena felt a tightening around her heart when she added, "Don't you see what I'm trying to do?"

"Honestly, no, I don't. Mainly because I know what I want and who I want, and let me tell you something else, Lena. I refuse for you or anyone else to decide my future for me." He crossed the room to the coatrack and got his jacket and slipped it on. "Come on, I'll walk you out."

Lena knew he was angry but she didn't know what else she could say or do to make him see reason. Why couldn't he understand that things needed to be back on a professional level be-. tween them?

When they reached her car, he asked before opening the door, "So what was tonight about, Lena?"

"I don't know what you mean."

"Yes, you do. Why did you let me make love to you tonight if you knew things would be over between us?"

When she didn't say anything he shook his head, understanding completely. "So it was one of those kinds of nights."

She raised her head and met his gaze. "What kind of nights?"

"Nothing but sex, pure sex and nothing but sex."

She cringed. His words had made it sound so dirty. "Why are you giving me a hard time about my decision, Morgan? I would think you would be overjoyed."

He stared at her before moving aside and opening the car door for her. "Yes, you would think that and you know what, Lena? I'm going to announce my candidacy without you or anyone else beside me."

When she got inside the car, she watched as he walked over to his own, and instead of getting in he stood there, staring at her. She held back the tears that threatened to fall. Why couldn't he see that everything she was doing was because she loved him?

"Let me get this straight," Kylie said, glaring at her best friend. "You actually told Morgan you couldn't marry him because he's decided to run for public office?"

Lena was glad they were the only two in the house. They were in the kitchen. She was sitting at the kitchen table when Kylie stood at the counter folding laundry.

Chance was out playing the usual Saturday morning basketball game with his brothers; Marcus and his latest girlfriend had left earlier for the mall, and Tiffany had gone to spend the weekend with her grandparents.

"Calm down, Kylie. I wouldn't want Chance to blame me if you went into labor early. And yes, I told him I couldn't marry him. It would not have been a real marriage anyway."

Kylie tossed the items she was about to fold back in the laundry basket and came and sat across the table from Lena. "And just what do you mean it would not have been a real marriage?"

Lena sighed. She knew that Kylie would be

upset because she had held all the facts of her pending engagement to Morgan from her. "First promise that you won't get mad."

Kylie rolled her eyes. "I won't promise you anything because I'm already mad. I can't believe you let Cassandra Tisdale and her band of Merry Hussies get to you."

"They didn't get to me."

"Sounds to me like they did. So let's get back on track. What do you mean that your marriage to Morgan would not have been real?"

Lena didn't say anything for a long time. Then she said, "Morgan and I entered into a business agreement."

Kylie lifted an arched brow. "What kind of business agreement?"

"I was to marry him and have his baby."

"What!"

"You heard me. He asked me to marry him just to have his baby."

Kylie stared at her for a long moment. And then she did the one thing Lena hadn't expected. She burst out laughing.

And she continued laughing to the point where Lena began getting slightly irritated. Personally, she didn't see anything funny, she thought, leaning back in her chair and crossing her arms over her chest and glaring across the table at Kylie. "Excuse me, I hate to interrupt, especially when I've evidently brought so much amusement into your life this morning, but can you please explain to me what the hell is so funny?"

Kylie stopped laughing, slightly. She then got up and went to the kitchen counter and grabbed a paper towel to dab at her eyes and said, "I'm so sorry, Lena, but Morgan pulled one over on you."

Lena's glare deepened. "Meaning?"

Kylie dabbed at her eyes some more and chuckled a few times before saying, "Meaning, he would have told you anything to get you married to him."

Lena inhaled deeply, still not knowing just what Kylie meant. "Kylie, I'm going to count to ten, and if you don't get that rump of yours back in this chair and tell me what you're talking about, then you will be going into labor early."

Kylie saw the threatening look in her eyes and knew her best friend meant business. "All right, all right," she said, coming back to sit down at the table.

"Now talk."

Kylie raised her eyes to the ceiling. "You're so smart I'm surprised you hadn't figured things out, Lena. Think," she said, reaching across the table and tapping a finger against what at the moment she considered her best friend's thick skull. "For months Morgan has been after you. He asked you out several times."

She glared at Kylie. "So? I'm sure he's asked several women out. Big deal."

"No, Lena. For Morgan it wasn't just a big deal. I think it almost became an obsession."

Lena frowned. "An obsession?"

"Yes. Not to the point that he would have resorted to stalking you or anything like that," Kylie said, grinning. "But he was determined to get you."

Lena considered Kylie's words for a moment, then asked softly, "In bed?"

Kylie immediately knew where Lena's thoughts were going and reached out and captured her hand. "No, Lena. I think it was more serious than that."

Lena's frown deepened. "What's more serious than a man going after a woman for the sole intent of getting her in his bed? And you knew about this and didn't tell me?"

Kylie shrugged. "I knew what Chance was telling me, which wasn't much, but enough to figure out what was going on. The reason I didn't tell you is that my husband asked me not to. He felt sooner or later sexual chemistry would do the both of you in. The brothers knew how bad Morgan wanted you, so they figured out why he'd hired you to sell his house and buy another."

Lena's eyes widened in startled shock. "Are you saying the reason Morgan hired me as a Realtor was that he wanted to sleep with me?"

Kylie rolled her eyes. "No, that's not what I'm saying, and will you please be quiet for a moment so I can give you my take on things?"

When Lena reluctantly nodded, she said, "My take on things is this. For Morgan it was more than having you in his bed. I honestly think he was quite taken with you, Lena, and he con-cocted this plan to get you right where he wanted you, as a permanent part of his life. Remember that day at lunch I told you about his belief about his *perfect* woman? In his mind you're it and he would have done anything for you to become a part of his life like he wanted to become a part of yours. But first he had to prove himself to you, let you see that he's not like those guys you dated before."

Lena bit her bottom lip. A part of her couldn't buy what Kylie was saying. Mainly because she couldn't see herself as any man's perfect anything. "I think you're wrong, Kylie."

"And I think I'm right, Lena. If all Morgan wanted was to sleep with you, once he'd done that he wouldn't have come back, and I know the two of you have slept together."

Lena leaned forward. "And how do you know that?"

Kylie smiled. "The same way you knew that Chance and I had slept together without me having said one word. I was celibate for over fifteen years and I know you haven't been with anyone since your dad died. Although I hadn't seen you in the past couple of days when I talked to you a couple of days ago you sounded funny."

Lena leaned back in the chair and lifted a brow. "Funny how?"

"Like you were tired, exhausted, sexually fulfilled. And when I talked to your mom yesterday and she happened to mentioned the fact that you had swollen lips, I thought that—"

Lena straightened in her chair. "Mom told you that?"

Kylie couldn't help but giggle. "Yes, you know mothers don't miss anything. They see everything. Trust me, although she might not have said anything, she noticed."

Lena nodded. "So what did you tell her?"

Kylie smiled. "I told her it must have been a soda bottle. I heard Donovan give that excuse to Chance once."

Lena inhaled deeply. "Okay, Morgan and I did sleep together, once."

Kylie lifted a brow, then reached out and touched a mark on Lena's upper arm. "Once? This sure looks like a recent passion mark to me."

Lena rolled her eyes. "Okay, more than once. So he got what he wanted."

Kylie shook her head. "I'm sorry you think that way. You know what your problem is, Lena?"

"No, what do you think my problem is, Kylie?" she asked sarcastically.

"I've known you all my life and you've always felt you've had to complete against skinny females. Why can't you believe and accept that there are some men who don't give a damn about a woman's weight? They see beyond all that and see what's in her heart. Why can't you believe Morgan is one of those men? To him, you are his perfect woman. You and not Jamie Hollis or any other slim woman who wants to catch his eye. But until you believe in your own beauty, both inside and outside, what he sees doesn't really matter."

* * *

Donovan glared at his two oldest brothers. "I refuse to play another game until the two of you calm Morgan down. What the hell is his problem?"

Bas smiled as he grabbed the ball from Chance. Morgan had called time-out for a bathroom break and they were using the time while he was gone to discuss him. "If I recall, you pissed him off that day when he was daydreaming in the meeting. You should have figured then there would be hell to pay. Stop whining and take it like a man."

"No, it's more than just that particular day," Chance said, concerned. "He's been playing pretty rough with all of us. I wonder what's going on."

"Whatever it is, I bet it has something to do with Lena," Donovan said.

Bas rolled his eyes. "What else is new?"

"Hey, look at who just walked in," Chance said.

Both Bas and Donovan squinted their eyes against the gym's bright lights. "Isn't that Jamie Hollis and your ex, Bas?" Donovan asked.

Bas frowned. "You make her sound like she used to be my wife," he said of the woman with Jamie, Cassandra Tisdale. "I wonder what the hell the two of them are doing here."

Donovan grinned. "Oh, I know the answer to

that one. Jamie is after Morgan. In fact there are bets going around that she's going to be the one he eventually marries instead of Lena."

Chance shook his head. "Does Morgan know that?"

"Yes, I told him. I also told him that I'd heard that Cassandra had even boasted about it to Lena," Donovan said.

"No wonder Lena dumped him," Bas said, frowning.

"Lena didn't dump me," Morgan said angrily, approaching his brothers from behind. "Ready to play another game?" He then glanced up into the bleachers, recognized the two women and frowned. "What the hell are they doing here?"

Bas turned to his brother and grinned. "Evidently, they came to see you get your ass kicked all over the basketball court today."

A few hours later Morgan was back at his place soaking in a hot tub of water. He and his brothers had played some pretty rough games today, but then he'd need the brutal workout to work out his frustrations. Now he could settle down and think.

He shook his head at the audacity of Cassandra and Jamie. They had tried their best to get him to agree to meet them some place for drinks and to play a game of tennis. He leaned back in the water thinking he wasn't stupid. He had seen that same look in Jamie Hollis's eyes that he'd seen in other women on a manhunt. She was a woman with a plan just like he had been a man with a plan. A plan that had backfired on him.

He wondered if Lena had figured things out yet and if she had, did she even care? Well, hell, he cared and if she thought he had given up on her she had another thought coming.

He got out of the tub and began drying off. Something Bas had said earlier piqued his interest. Evidently Lena was a part of Vanessa's latest community project, and there would be a meeting at her house sometime this evening. There was no reason for him not to stop by and give his regards to the ladies.

Vanessa Steele rolled her eyes at the man standing on her doorstep. "What are you doing here, Morgan?"

He smiled. "Do I need a reason to visit one of my favorite cousins?"

She frowned. "No, but it does seem odd since you haven't been over here since Christmas."

He chuckled. "Only because the last time I dropped by you told me not to come back."

Her frown deepened. "I told you not to come back if you had to bring Cameron Cody with you. That man is not welcome in my home."

Morgan shook his head. "Wasn't it just last Sunday that Pastor Givens spoke about forgiveness?"

She lifted an arched brow. "I'm surprised you remembered the sermon since you, Donovan and Bas usually fall asleep during service. It's a sin and a shame."

"No need to get ugly about it." He shoved away from the wall. "So, are you going to invite me in or not?"

Vanessa stared at him as if she was considering his question, and then she moved aside. "Only because Dane's going to drop Sienna off and he might hang around if you're here."

Morgan entered the house and glanced around, heard feminine voices coming from the back and smiled when he heard one in particular. He then turned to Vanessa and asked, "Why does Dane have to drive Sienna over here?"

Vanessa couldn't stop the smile that spread across her lips. "Because they're driving to Memphis right after the meeting to spend the weekend." She leaned closer and whispered, "Sienna has some special news for Dane."

Morgan nodded. From the way Vanessa had said it, he had an idea just what that news was. He then thought of Lena and the day she would tell him some special news. But first he knew he had to win her over. First he had to get the wife, and then the baby.

"Well, ladies, look who just showed up," Vanessa said to the three women in her kitchen.

Everyone turned and stared at Morgan, but it was Lena who held his gaze the longest. "Hello, everyone. I just decided to pay Vanessa a visit, so don't mind me," he said.

Jocelyn, who was still trying to get to know her husband's family, smiled over at him and said, "It's good seeing you, Morgan."

"Same here, Jocelyn." He then glanced over at Kylie. "And how are you, Kylie, besides pregnant?"

She made a face at him before saying, "Fine and counting. One more month to go and I'm free."

He nodded. He then crossed the room to Lena. She was standing alone near the sink. Remembering their last conversation he wasn't sure how her attitude would be toward him. "Hello, Lena."

"Morgan."

"How's your mother?"

"She's doing fine. Thanks for asking."

He nodded. "I told Vanessa I would make myself useful while I'm here. I'll be outside trimming her hedges if you need me for anything."

She lifted a brow. "If I need you for anything?"

He smiled. "Yes."

Lena stared at him, remembering what Kylie had told her just that morning. The only reason Morgan had hired her to sell his house was that he had wanted her, although she and Kylie had a difference of opinion of just what the word *want* actually meant.

"I'm glad you came here today since I was going to seek you out tomorrow."

She watched the smile spread to his eyes. "You were?"

"Yes. There's something I needed to tell you, and if you have time, since the meeting hasn't started yet, maybe I can do it now."

His smile widened. "Sure. Let's go into Vanessa's study for privacy."

Lena nodded and then glanced around the room at the other ladies, not surprised to find them staring at her and Morgan. Evidently there weren't too many secrets in the Steele family. Had all of them known of his obsession to have her in his bed? "If you'll excuse me for a moment, I need to speak with Morgan about something."

She followed Morgan to Vanessa's study, and the moment the door was closed, she inhaled deeply, feeling angry and frustrated.

He leaned back on Vanessa's desk and smiled at her. "So, what did you want to talk to me about?"

She crossed the room, trying to hold back her anger and the hurt she felt. "It has come to my attention that you hired me as your real estate agent for an indecent reason and I just want you to know that effective today, I quit."

Then without saying anything else, she turned and walked out of the room.

Chapter 16

On Monday morning Morgan was standing at the window in his office thinking about what Lena had told him on Saturday. Since the meeting had started he hadn't gotten a chance to talk to her after that because as soon as the meeting was over she'd left.

But then, what exactly could he have said? He couldn't deny that he'd had ulterior motives for hiring her as a Realtor. But she was wrong about any of it being indecent.

He was in love with her, but he knew he would

have a hard time convincing her of that now. He had talked to Kylie yesterday and she had convinced him that the best thing to do was to just give Lena time to come around. Well, he didn't want to give her time. He wanted and needed her like he needed his next breath.

His secretary's voice on the intercom intruded into his thoughts.

"Yes, Linda?"

"There's a Ms. Jamie Hollis here to see you. She doesn't have an appointment but indicated she's Senator Hollis's daughter."

Morgan rolled his eyes. Like he gave a flip, and he was ready to tell Linda to advise the senator's daughter he was too busy to see her. But then he decided what the hell? He needed to set Jamie straight once and for all. "All right, Linda, please send her in."

A few minutes later Jamie walked in with her expensive perfume almost choking him. She was dressed in an outfit that probably cost a pretty penny, and she looked the epitome of a wealthy, sophisticated, aristocratic lady. He had to admit she was an attractive woman, but he was able to see beyond that beauty to someone he wouldn't be attached to even for a billion dollars. "Jamie," he said, with a forced smile, crossing the room to give her a formal handshake. "What can I do for you?"

She smiled up at him as she took the seat he offered. "The question, Morgan, is what I can do for you. I'd like to make you an offer I don't think you'll be able to refuse."

He lifted a brow and leaned back on his desk. "Really, and what is it?"

"A partnership between us."

He inwardly shuddered, wondering if that's how he'd sounded that day he had offered Lena a business deal between them. If so, then he regretted every word he'd spoken. "What kind of a partnership?"

"Marriage. I'll be thirty this time next year, and Daddy thinks it's time I do something."

Morgan crossed his arms over his chest. "Does he?"

"Yes. And I was bred and groomed to be a politician's wife, someone who's going places. And I want to become a mother one day, with a nanny of course."

She shifted in the chair, and her smile widened and excitement shone in her eyes as she continued. "Everyone sees you as a top contender for Charlotte's first black mayor in a few years, and who knows where that will lead? I could see you as the governor, even president one day. And I intend to be your First Lady all the way."

Like hell you will. He cleared his throat. Evidently she had erroneously thought things through. "I appreciate your offer, Jamie, but I thought you knew."

"Knew what?"

"I've asked someone else to marry me. In fact we'll be announcing our engagement sometime this week."

The spark in her eyes was replaced with a furious dart. "Really? Who?"

"Lena Spears."

She blinked and then he watched a smile touch her lips before she waved her well-manicured, neatly polished hand in the air like his words had held no significant meaning. "Really? Morgan, Lena is not the woman you need, I am. In fact after our little talk last week with Lena, Cassandra and I were sure we had convinced her that if she cared anything for you she would get out of the picture."

He straightened. "Excuse me?"

"I said we had a talk with Lena last week. We happened to run into her at McIntosh's. She's a very sensible woman who I believes loves you, but we made it quite clear that she wasn't the woman for you. For a man of your caliber, you need a woman who possesses style, grace, pedigree, wealth and connections."

Morgan shook his head. "Let me get this straight. You actually said those things to Lena?"

She smiled. "Of course. Someone needed to be honest and up front with her. And since the two of you hadn't announced an engagement this weekend, I assumed she took our advice."

Morgan nodded. *She had.* No wonder she had given him that garbage that night in her office about not being the appropriate woman for him. He walked over to the chair Jamie was sitting in and leaned over, placing his hands on the arms and pinning her in. Anger, the likes he'd never known before, flowed through him.

"Listen, Jamie, and listen well," he said through gritted teeth. "There will never be a business partnership of any kind between us. When I marry, I will marry for love, and the woman I marry will be Lena Spears. And I will be marrying her for all the right reasons, and if I ever hear of you or anyone else spouting anything to her about not being good enough for me and my political future, you will have to deal with me. Do you understand?"

"Are you threatening me, Morgan?"

"No, I'm telling it like it is, and if you ever

come back I will get on television and tell everyone about why it was necessary for you to take that trip to London for six months last year."

She blinked. "What are you talking about?"

"You figure it out. But like you, I do have connections and mine talk and have all the proof we need. It would be an embarrassment not only for your father but also for the Tisdale family, who think so highly of their family name."

He'd said enough. Cameron, who made it a point to keep tabs on people who could either be a menace or someone useful to him in the future, had picked up wind of the senator's daughter's pregnancy and how she'd gone to London to give the child up for adoption. He had found it interesting and had passed the information on to Morgan earlier that year.

He stepped back, more than certain she was ready to leave his office and wouldn't be coming back any time soon. Before she walked out the door he said, "And if I were you I would try and find a way to convince Cassandra to keep her mouth shut, too. There's a lot she doesn't want taken out of her closet as well."

He walked back to the window and didn't even look around when he heard the door slam shut.

* * *

After lunch Morgan placed a call to a friend from college who happened to be the top anchorwoman at the city's leading television station. When Gail Winston came on the line he said, "All right, Gail, I promised you first dibs when I decided to run for office."

He laughed and placed the phone away from his ear when he heard her scream. "Yes, I'd like to announce it on your show Friday morning, but there's a catch."

He knew that would grab her attention. "Listen up. This is how I want you to handle things."

Gail Winston smiled into the camera. It was Friday morning and in a few seconds another segment of her local morning talk show would begin. When the producer gave her cue, she began.

"First, I want to thank our next guests who have joined forces with our local high schools to present a career fair that will be held next week. We have with us today Vanessa Steele, PR representative for the Steele Corporation. Lena Spears, a local Realtor from our area. And Jocelyn Steele, who will be the general manager of Cody Construction here in town. And it's my understanding Cody

Construction will be establishing apprenticeship training in the areas of bricklaying, air-conditioning and plumbing this fall for individuals who are interested in those occupations."

Putting an even bigger smile on her face, Gail said, "Good morning, ladies."

"Good morning," the three women said simultaneously.

And for the next ten minutes, under the direction of Gail's intense questions, they talked to the television audience about the importance of the students in the area coming out and taking part in such a worthwhile event.

After a commercial break, Gail came back on the air with the three ladies still sitting with her onstage in guest seats. "The reason I asked these ladies to remain is that two of them are members of the Steele family. And it just so happens that we have a surprise guest for everyone today. For years it's been speculated that sooner or later one of this city's favorite sons would enter politics, and today history is in the making. I have as our special guest someone most of you know because of his involvement in so many community affairs. Let's give a warm welcome to Morgan Steele, director of research and development for the Steele Corporation."

The audience applauded when Morgan walked out onstage and took the extra guest seat, which just happened to be beside Lena. Lena's heart almost stopped when he walked out. Impeccably dressed in a dark suit, white shirt and red tie, he looked like a movie celebrity rather than a businessman and easily took the breath away of any female seeing him.

She tried to focus her gaze on the monitor and not on him, for fear of another heartbreak. She loved him, and wooing her had been nothing more than a game to him.

Morgan settled into his seat. He hoped like hell this plan worked and had felt confident that it would, but now he wasn't all that sure, especially with the tension he could feel radiating from Lena.

Gail took control and pulled in his attention.

"Morgan has been a guest on my show before to promote numerous community causes, but this time he's here for another reason, right, Morgan?"

He smiled into the camera. "Right, Gail. Today I want to officially announce my candidacy for the council-at-large seat here in Charlotte. However, there is one condition."

Gail leaned forward and smiled. "And what condition is that?" she dutifully asked.

"I am a single man and there are a group of

people who believe it's important that I have a good woman by my side, and I agree. What I don't agree with is the theory that I should choose a woman because the public thinks she and I will do well together politically as a team."

The camera angled in on him, and the intensity in his features couldn't be missed as he continued. "The woman I will marry is a woman I trust, a woman I know will have my back no matter what, and a woman I know is capable of being everything I could ever want in a wife. She is also a woman I love. I don't care if some people out there think she's not what they want for me. She is the woman I want for myself."

He paused for a second, then said, "So many times when people are involved in politics, they marry for all the wrong reasons. They form a partnership instead of a real marriage, and that's not what I want for myself. I could not understand the importance of the family and marriage dynamics if I didn't have a real marriage of my own. I want to marry for love and nothing else."

Anyone listening to what Morgan had said, whether a romantic or not, had to have felt the deep emotions he'd just conveyed in his words. Even Gail dabbed at her eyes.

"So, have you asked this young lady to marry you yet?" Gail couldn't help asking since she knew her audience would want to know.

"Yes, but at the time I asked her for the wrong reason. Now I want to ask her for the right one. I want her to know how much I truly do love her and that more than anything I want her to be my wife and the mother of my children. And whether I win this election bid doesn't matter as long as I have her by my side and in my life."

Gail dabbed at her eyes again. "Do you think she's out there watching the show and knows what you're saying?"

"It's even better than that," he said, smiling. "The woman I love just happens to be here onstage with us." Then before anyone could blink, Morgan got out of his chair and on his knees in front of Lena, while pulling a small white velvet box out of his pants pocket.

The cameras moved in closer, determined to capture the entire thing on film. Morgan took Lena's hand in his and gazed up into her eyes and took a deep breath. "Lena, if there is anything such as love at first sight, then it happened to me the night of the American Cancer Society's annual ball, when you walked into that ballroom. I can remember in full detail the dress you were wearing that night because you were such a vision of beauty in it that it took my breath away. And I knew from that night on I had to make you mine.

"And I'm here before you, on bended knee, wanting to do that. I love you and I believe you love me, too. Otherwise you would not have cared what became of my future. But what you don't know is that I truly don't have a future without you. You are the essence of my very being. You are the woman I want to see when I wake up in the morning, and the last face I want to see before going to sleep at night. You are the only woman I want and need in my life. You are my perfect woman. You are my everything."

His smile wavered just a little when he saw all her tears. He hoped they weren't tears of sadness but tears of joy. He opened the ring box and held the ring in his hand. "And will you make me the happiest man on earth, sweetheart, by agreeing to marry me? Will you marry me, Lena, and have my babies, to stick beside me for better or worse, richer or poorer, sickness and in health, until death do us part?"

Tears continued to stream down Lena's face.

The man she loved more than anything was proclaiming his love for her for all to hear. It was only when everything in the studio got quiet, except for the sounds of more than a few sniffles, that she realized that everyone, especially Morgan, was waiting on her answer.

She leaned forward and cupped his face in her hand. Meeting his gaze she said, loud and clear, "And I love you, too, Morgan, and yes, I will marry you and have your babies. And you will make me an extremely happy woman as well."

Morgan slid the ring on Lena's hand, and of course the cameraman had to slide his camera over for the ultimate shot for the television audience.

"Can you believe the size of that rock?" Gail exclaimed to everyone as the monitor continued to zero in on Lena's hand.

"Well, folks, this is certainly a first. I don't know of any other morning show where someone can officially announce their candidacy and do a marriage proposal in the same ten-minute segment."

Everyone heard her words, but most people were staring at Morgan when he stood to his feet and pulled Lena into his arms for one whopper of a kiss.

Gail smiled brightly, knowing her ratings would soar. "Well, there you have it, folks. A man who puts love before any political career he might be seeking certainly will definitely get my vote. And remember you saw it live right here."

Lena smiled tremendously as she glanced around the room. "Are you sure this is the house you want, Morgan? Your other home was—"

"My other home. I want to start somewhere new with you and Odessa. I knew when you showed this house to me that day that it would be perfect for us and our family."

She nodded happily as she walked into his outstretched arms. "What about your other home? Does Donovan still want it?"

Morgan threw his head back and chuckled. "Honey, Donovan never wanted my house. I talked him into buying it as part of my plan to get you."

Lena shook her head. "And you were that desperate?"

"Yes, for you I was that desperate. Plan A failed badly, but I was determined to make plan B a success. I hit a few bumps along the way but in the end I got you just where I want you, in my arms."

She cocked her head back and looked at him. "And not your bed."

He grinned. "Yes, there, too."

Lena moved closer and placed her head on her fiancé's chest. Today had to be the happiest day of her life. "Thanks for making sure Mom and everyone at the adult day care center was able to see this morning's show. She was so proud."

Morgan smiled. "And I'm glad. She's a part of out family and I never want her to forget it."

Lena leaned back in his arms to look up at him. Tears shone in her eyes. "Thanks That means a lot to me."

"I know it, sweetheart. And because it means a lot to you it means a lot to me as well. And you know the question everyone will be asking. When is our wedding date?"

Lena sighed. "I always wanted a June wedding, but so did Kylie and Jocelyn and they never got one."

Morgan smiled. "Only because my impatient brothers couldn't wait. Luckily for you, June is only three months away. It might kill me but I'll wait."

She leaned back and kissed his chin. "Thanks. Morgan. You are a wonderful man."

He chuckled. "Yeah, and don't you ever forget it. And I have a wonderful idea."

"What?"

"Let's christen our new home right now."

Lena grinned. She had an idea just how he wanted that particular ceremony done. "But it doesn't have any furniture."

"You think not? Then come with me."

Morgan took Lena's hand and led her up the stairs and toward the master suite that connected to the main house by a glass breezeway and elevator access. "Now close your eyes," he said.

Lena did as he demanded and felt him tug her along. Moments later he said, "You can open them now."

She gasped after opening her eyes. The master suite was completely furnished. She glanced around, not believing the beauty and the workmanship of the furniture. "But how? Who?"

Morgan grinned as he drew her to him again. "I left the decorating up to Sienna. We've always considered her the Steeles' personal interior decorator. And Reese Singleton, Jocelyn's brother-in-law, built the furniture by hand. I commissioned him to start building it last summer when I went to Newton Grove, and he, Bas, Donovan and I went on a fishing trip together one weekend. I'd seen his work and knew I wanted him to design our bedroom furniture. I didn't know at the time just how I was going to get you to become a permanent part of my life, but I intended to do whatever I had to do to succeed."

Lena laughed as she glanced around at the beautiful furniture and decorating. He even had decorative blinds up to the windows. Everything was simply elegant. "But who gave you permission to put furniture in here? You haven't purchased this place yet."

Morgan shook his head, grinning. "Technically I have. When my Realtor quit on me last weekend," he said with a teasing glint in his eyes, "I decided I had to do what I needed to do. I used the company's attorney to close the deal, but with the understanding that my Realtor would still get the commission."

Lena shook her head. Morgan had basically thought of everything. "And I guess it was your idea for Mom to be invited over to Chance and Kylie's place for the night, right?"

He laughed. "Right."

Lena looked up at the ceiling. "What am I going to do with you, Morgan Steele?"

"Love me. Marry me and have my babies?" He leaned forward and captured her lips with his. The moment his tongue touched hers she felt fire light up inside her. And then the seduction began.

Lena had discovered that Morgan was skilled at whatever he did. And when it came to multitasking, he was at the top of the list. He began stroking her back, grinding the lower part of his body against her spread thighs, rubbing his chest against the taut tips of her breasts, while kissing her senseless. She closed her eyes and moaned like a woman in dire need of her man.

All she could think about and all she wanted to focus on were being in that bed with him, him making love to her, and having him inside her. He pulled back and whispered in her ear, "Undress for me, baby."

She smiled, liking the idea of stripping for him. She took a step back to slide the blouse over her head and skimmed the skirt she was wearing down her hips, leaving her clad only in a royal-blue thong. She placed her hands on her hips and smiled at him. "So, what do you think?"

He returned her smile. "I'd rather show you than tell you."

Quickly, he begin removing all of his clothes with a wicked grin plastered to his face. In no time at all he was standing in front of her, completely naked, but he saw she had one remaining piece left on. Her thong.

His smile widened as he got down on his knees in front of her. "I see you save the best for last."

She balanced her hands on his shoulders while he slowly slid the thin wispy material down her legs. And just like she'd known he would do, once it was removed he leaned forward and attached his mouth to her womanly core, giving her one hell of a tongue-lashing kiss there. She had to grip his shoulders to keep her balance, and when an orgasm hit her she screamed his name.

Moments later he stood, smiled and took her hand in his. "That was just an appetizer. Come on, sweetheart, let's christen our bed."

Morgan's groin tightened as he watched Lena ease her naked body into the huge bed. *Perfect,* he thought, easing onto the bed behind her, like a lion stalking his prey. And then he had her in his arms, kissing her deeply, with all the love in his heart.

Lena gazed up at him when he positioned his body over hers, and she knew this would be a moment she would remember for the rest of her life. Today on television he had asked her to marry him, and now in the beautiful home he had purchased for her he was about to make her his in the most elemental way.

"I love you, Morgan," she whispered.

He smiled down at her. "And I love you, too. For always."

And then he eased his body into hers, closed his eyes and locked in place for a moment to absorb the intensity of the moment and to thank God for sending such a beautiful woman into his life. He then opened his eyes at the same time his body began to move. Sexual need combined with every deep emotion he possessed took over, and he established a rhythm that immediately sent all kinds of shudders racing through him.

"Lena!"

He was hit by the strongest force that could ever take down a man and literally bring him to his knees. The force of love. And he lifted her hips as another orgasm hit, and when he felt her body shattering as well he screamed out her name yet again.

And he knew what the two of them were sharing went beyond temptation. It went beyond anything he knew. And it would set the stage for the wonderful love they would always share. Together.

Epilogue

A beautiful day in June

"You may kiss your bride, Morgan."

Those were the very words Morgan had been waiting for, although he felt it had taken Reverend Givens long enough to say them. As far as he was concerned this had to have been the longest wedding ceremony on record. But as he glanced down at the beautiful woman in front of him, he knew it had been well worth it and more.

He pulled her into his arms and captured her lips in his, making another promise; one only the two of them understood. Today would begin the rest of their lives together and tonight they intended to start work on their dynasty. She had gone off the Pill months ago and tonight he would start another mission.

He pulled back when he felt a jab to his ribs and knew it had to have been Bas. Evidently the kiss had lasted longer than some people felt it should have. He smiled down into Lena's beautiful smiling face. "I love you, Mrs. Steele."

She smiled back up at him with tears shining in her eyes. "And I love you, Mr. Steele."

They turned to their audience, all five hundred of their guests, and smiled as the pastor announced proudly, "I now present to everyone, Morgan and Lena Steele."

Morgan shot a glance over at Cameron, who had served as one of his groomsmen. He then looked at his cousin Vanessa, who didn't look like a happy camper. He chuckled. He would give Cameron at least until the end of the summer to finally win his stubborn cousin over.

But Morgan knew he himself had other things

to worry about. Making his wife happy, making a baby, and starting his campaign at full force. He had a lot to accomplish.

But of course like always, he was a man with a plan.

About the Author

Brenda Jackson is a die "heart" romantic who married her childhood sweetheart and still proudly wears the "going steady" ring he gave her when she was fifteen. Because she's always believed in the power of love, Brenda's stories always have happy endings. In her real-life love story, Brenda and her husband of thirty-four years live in Jacksonville, Florida and have two sons.

A USA Today Bestselling author of over forty romance titles, Brenda divides her time between family, writing and working in management at a major insurance company. You may write Brenda at P.O Box 28267, Jacksonville, Florida 32226; her e-mail address at WriterBJackson@aol.com, or visit her website at www.brendajackson.net

A brand-new story of love
and drama from...

national bestselling author

MARCIA
KING-GAMBLE

Big-boned beauty Chere Adams
plunges into an extreme makeover
to capture the eye of fitness fanatic
Quentin Abraham—but the more
she changes, the less he seems to
notice her. Is it possible Quentin's
more interested in the old Chere?

*Available the first week of January
wherever books are sold.*

KIMANI
ROMANCE

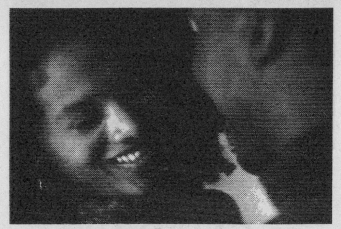

Big-boned beauty, Chere Adams
plunges headfirst into an
extreme makeover to impress
fitness fanatic
Quentin Abrahams.

But perhaps it's Chere's curves that
have caught Quentin's eye?

All About Me

Marcia
King-Gamble

AVAILABLE JANUARY 2007
FROM KIMANI™ ROMANCE

Love's Ultimate Destination